MURDER

of

Cowboy

Gene

Jay Heavner

Canaveral Publishing

D1452453

All the author's books can be obtained at Amazon

Braddock's Gold Novels

Braddock's Gold

Hunter's Moon

Fool's Wisdom

Killing Darkness

Florida Murder Mystery Novels

Death at Windover

Murder at the Canaveral Diner

Murder at the Indian River

Murder at Seminole Pond

Murder of Cowboy Gene

Dedication

To

Sarah

Acknowledgments

Special thanks to my wife, Vivian

for suggestions, proofing, support, and edition.

Thanks, William Rowland, for first proofing.

Special thanks to all my first readers,

Sandra A. Smith,

Rene Hunt,

Marie Waters Clyde,

Cindy Moran, and

Lora Sargent

Murder of Cowboy Gene

Chapter 1

Spring, 1984,

East Coast Central Florida

If Carole had known she was going to be robbed that day, she'd have worn a nice dress; one that made her look good, but it had been the bank's newly created casual day. Instead, she'd worn some tight jeans that accentuated her still trim figure and a University of Florida T-shirt with the team mascot, Albert E. Gator, probably named after the character in the Pogo comic strip, on the front. Her oldest son, Harry, named after his dad, went to school in Gainesville, majoring in partying and girl-chasing. One day he'd have to pick a major and stick with it.

No, the robbery had been nothing like she could have imagined. It did put a little excitement into her mundane life. Many of the dreams she had when younger she'd put on hold years ago. Maybe someday, she'd get another chance to pursue them. Maybe when the kids were gone, and she and Harold were empty nesters. Harold was the man who'd swept her off her feet, and she'd married. It had been a whirlwind courtship with a quick marriage and a child seven months later.

She'd always thought a bank robbery would be more spectacular. The thieves, all big burly men wearing masks and carrying powerful military-grade weapons, would storm through the front door, fire bursts from their guns into the ceiling, scream profanities, and order everyone down on the floor. One false move and all would die. Then they'd force the bank manager to open the vault and take everything they could carry out in large duffle bags while firing more rounds into the ceiling as they ran out screaming that no one better follow them or call the cops. Tires would squeal, and smoke would billow when they left yards of rubber on the road as they thundered away, running people off the highway and blowing through red lights and stop signs.

No, it wasn't like that. It had been somewhat disappointing, as was her life today. No one had even noticed anything out of the ordinary when the slim man moderate in height, five foot eight, she guessed, walked into the bank, and patiently waited in the short line. She'd greeted him as he came to her teller's place. There was nothing unusual about him. He wore a cowboy hat, a Stetson, she thought but wasn't sure. She'd seen lots of them on the men who used the bank. Some were local ranchers, and some just liked that style of hat.

He had a well-trimmed beard, gray-white, and a little hint of the same color in the hair around his temples. Again, nothing out of the norm. A flannel shirt, blue jeans, and cowboy boots finished out what he wore. She noticed a little roll around his middle. Seemed all men about that age had one of those. And large sunglasses with a medium tint. She'd almost forgotten about those.

He didn't seem the least bit anxious as she thought all bank robbers would be. He never spoke, and his eyes, what little she could see, showed more curiosity than malice to her. Calmly, he'd handed her a note. *This is a robbery. Give me lots of money. No die packs. No marked bills. I know where you live. No one needs to get hurt. Just do as you're told. Thank you for your cooperation.*

The bank had trained her how to deal with robbers, but his calmness and lack of nervousness put her at ease. Was she really being robbed? Could it be this easy and nonthreatening?

After reading the note, she looked up, and his face told her he was serious. He handed her a medium size bag, which she filled and gave it back to him. At that point, she noticed he was wearing gloves. He took the bag in his left hand, tipped his hat slightly, winked at her, she thought, though it was hard to tell with the sunglasses on, and casually walked out of the bank, never looking back.

It wasn't until the next person walked to her teller booth and asked why she looked confused that she fully realized she'd been robbed and told him so. He looked puzzled. Coming to her senses, Carole told the bank manager what had happened, and the alarm was sounded.

The police came quickly, but the robber was long gone by then. They searched the area but found nothing.

He'd vanished. They closed the bank and looked for evidence but found none.

A detective came and interviewed everyone there, with Carole being his last person. He listened patiently to her story, asked a few questions, and occasionally nodded his head while writing notes. After she'd told her story to him a second time, he'd asked her to go over it again. He exhaled deeply and said, "Sounds like the work of Cowboy Gene."

Carole smiled. This mundane robbery had gotten interesting. She'd been afraid her robbery experience had been a dud, not worth telling. Still, everybody knew about Cowboy Gene, the notorious gentleman bank robber who vanished like a ghost and had driven the cops crazy trying to catch him for years on end. Her grin grew wider. She'd been robbed by a legend. Maybe they'd even mention her name in the *Florida Today* newspaper.

After the interview, the police sent everyone home, except the manager. The bank would be closed for the rest of the day while they looked for evidence they'd overlooked, if any. They viewed the surveillance tapes from inside and outside of the bank. Yup, it had to be Cowboy Gene, no doubt about that, and as usual, he just disappeared from sight walking, never getting into a car they could identify and track him down. Cowboy Gene had done it again, robbed another bank and got away scot-free. They could add one more to his long list. Someday, he'd slip up, make a mistake, and they'd catch him, but today didn't seem to be the day.

Nevertheless, Carole had a great story, and she told everybody who would listen, and a few that really didn't want to, about her adventure today. She went over every detail with her husband after supper. Why she was somebody. She'd been robbed by the infamous Cowboy Gene.

That night, she was the aggressive one in the bedroom. It was a night Harold would remember for a long time, and secretly he hoped that Cowboy Gene would rob her again and again and again if only to put more little thrills into their mundane lives. It sure had done so that day.

He woke early the next day and made her breakfast in bed. Afterward, they made love over and over, and both were late for work, but neither regretted it. It had been worth all the money Cowboy Gene had stolen, and besides, it wasn't their money anyway. They hoped the legend of Cowboy Gene would continue. Maybe if they were lucky, he really would pay the bank a second visit, soon.

Chapter 2

Fall 1960

"Stop here. I see one sticking his nose out of the bushes."

Mandy did as her younger sister had asked. "Peggy Sue, how you can see and find them is beyond me."

"It's a gift, Mandy. I like lost and forgotten things."

"You got a big heart, Peggy Sue, bigger than your purse. There's no way we can keep and feed all these animals."

"I know, but I can try. I can do what I can. Maybe I can make a difference for some of them. Now, you be real quiet, but beep the horn if you see trouble. Not everyone out here has good intentions."

"How well I know that. See if you can catch that one."

Ten-year-old Peggy Sue got out of the 1951 Chevrolet Deluxe coupe her fifteen-year-old sister drove. Mandy was getting good at using the clutch and rarely ever raked the gears, but sometimes she had trouble with the three on the tree shifter.

The small frightened dog ran into the woods. Mandy watched as Peggy Sue tried to coax the skinny dog back. "Hey, little boy," she said. "I got this piece of hot dog just for you. You look hungry, and it's just for you, but you got to come and get it. I won't hurt you. Come on, little boy."

Mandy watched as her sister continued to try to talk the dog out of the scrubby Brazilian Pepper bushes. "Here you go, little boy. Come on." She bent over. "Damn," she said.

"What's wrong, sis?"

"Almost had him, but he got away. Maybe the hot dog will take his hunger away for a while. He's way back in the bushes, and I can't even see him."

"Don't you go back there after him. You remember what happened last week, Peggy Sue."

How well she did. A bum hiding in the brush had grabbed her, and it took everything the two girls had to fight him off. A stiff kick by Mandy to the man's groin had taken all the fight out of him. It had scared the girls something plenty. Mandy wanted to quit their animal rescue, but Peggy Sue had managed to talk her out of quitting. They just needed to be more careful, she said. Neither one wanted to repeat that incident.

Peggy Sue got back in the car. "I almost had him. I was so close. Damn."

"Mom'll get mad if she hears you talking like that."

"Mandy, I've heard you say that word and worse."

"That's different."

"Why's it different?"

"'Cause I'm your big sister, that's why." Mandy got her younger sister in a headlock and ran her knuckles over Peggy Sue's head.

"Ouch," hollered Peggy Sue. "That hurts."

"Naw, that's just a big sister keeping her little sister in line. I could really hurt you if I wanted."

"You wouldn't hurt me, really, would you?"

"Naw, I wouldn't. You know better than that." She gave Peggy Sue a hug. The younger girl hugged her back. After a few moments, they separated.

Peggy Sue slid across the seat, crossed her arms, and looked out the window. "Life's not fair."

"No, it's not."

"Why can't everything have a home and someone who loves them? Why do people have to fight and steal?" She paused and turned to her sister. "And why did Daddy have to die?"

Mandy said nothing for a moment. "I wish I knew the answers to those questions, Peggy Sue, but I don't. I wish I knew." She exhaled heavily. "Daddy got cancer, and it ate him up. Mom thinks he got into something toxic in the war, but she can't prove it, and the army says his records of his activities when he liberated the work camp are still classified, and they won't let her see them."

"But how's a man get breast cancer? Guys don't even have boobs. It's not fair."

"I know, sis. Mom said it's rare in men, but it does happen. Would you have been happier if he died in a car wreck or on his job?"

Peggy Sue thought about it. "No, guess it doesn't really matter. He could have gotten the flu or some other terrible bug and died. But it still ain't fair."

"No, it's not. Mom said you just gotta go on and make the best of it."

"You really believe that, Mandy?"

"It does seem kinda simple and hokey, but I don't have anything any better, and I know it keeps Mom going when she could quit like some people do, have a pity party, and ruin their lives and those who depend on them."

Peggy Sue said, "When you put it that way, it kinda makes sense. I don't know what we'd do without Mom."

"She works hard at her job and tries to provide for us best she can."

"Mandy, are we poor?"

"Hell's bells, yes, little sister, but everyone in this town is poor as church mice, so it don't make any difference, does it?

"Guess not. Mandy, when I grow up, somehow I'm gonna have money. I think it would be nice not to be poor."

"Yeah, I think it would be nice to not have to worry about money, but how would a couple of poor white girls like us get some big money?"

Peggy Sue said, "Maybe we could get an education or something. Maybe we could rob banks. They got lots of money and wouldn't miss the little we'd take."

Mandy rolled her eyes. "Peggy Sue, where do you get these crazy ideas? Mom would beat your bottom if she heard you talking like this."

"Mom would beat your bottom, too, if she knew what you and Billy were doing."

Mandy's face drained. "You keep your mouth shut on that. Mom don't need to know."

"Are you using protection? I know what happens if you don't."

A look of surprise crossed Mandy's face. She grimaced and looked out the window. Her little sister knew too much. "Yes, we're taking precautions, so nothing happens. Now, you're not gonna tell Mom, are you?"

"No, it's a sister secret. Kinda like those classified secrets of the government."

Mandy smiled, "Yeah, a sister secret, like double top secret."

"Or higher," Peggy Sue said.

"Or higher," Mandy repeated, relieved. "I think we've had enough today. I better get this Chevy back before Mom notices it's not parked at the house."

"Yeah, thanks, sis, for helping me with my animal rescue operation."

"You're welcome. And mum's the word on what we talked about, right?"

"Yup, sister secrets are like that."

Chapter 3

Spring 1984

"Peggy Sue, could you please come here? I need some help."

"Just a minute, Mom. I'm in the bathroom."

"Okay. It's not an emergency."

Peggy Sue finished up her business and pulled up her pants. She washed her hands and quickly dried them. As she headed out the bathroom door, she said, "I'm coming, Mom," but heard no response.

She quickly walked to her mother's room and found her sitting in her overstuffed chair. "Are you okay, Mom?"

"I'm stuck. Could you help me get up? I have to go."

"Sure thing, Mom." Good-hearted Peggy Sue slipped her hand under her mother's armpit and helped her to her feet.

Mom smiled. "Seems like I'm having more of these, Peggy Sue. Getting old sure isn't for sissies. Get out and do what you need to do while you're still young. I feel like an anchor holding you down, keeping you here."

"It's okay, Mom. What kind of child would I be if I didn't take care of my mother in her old age? Besides, I'm making plans for the future. What I need today is just to take care of what needs to be taken care of today. Simple as that."

"Bless you, daughter. If only your brother and sister felt the same way."

"Mom, we've been over this before. Sis has her own family issues she's dealing with, and my brother's busy with his business. He makes sure we don't need nothin' and visits on Sunday when he can. It may not be perfect, but it's working out."

"Peggy Sue, I just feel like I'm a burden for you."

"Mom, it's okay." She kissed her on the cheek. "I love you, Mom."

Mom smiled. "Peggy Sue, what would I do without you?"

"Mom, didn't you have to go?"

"Yeah, I better do that. Don't need any puddles on the floor."

Peggy Sue helped her mother into the bathroom. Mom pulled up her dress, dropped her white cotton pants, grabbed a silver handicap bar, and sat down.

Mom said, "It may take a little while. I'll call you if I need help. Why don't you go get us some breakfast?"

"Okay, Mom. You know to call if you need help."

"Sure thing. Eggs would be fine."

"Scrambled or sunny-side up like you like them?"

"Peggy Sue, I think I'm feeling adventurous today. Let's go with scrambled."

"Sure thing, Mom."

Peggy Sue left the bathroom, washed her hands in the kitchen sink, got Mr. Coffee brewing, and began fixing breakfast. She cut up a small onion, a pepper, and a sausage and added them to the eggs cooking in the iron skillet. A little shredded cheddar cheese topped off the omelet. She turned off the electric eye to the stove as it finished cooking. Cinnamon raisin bread, two pieces, was added to the toaster. She heard her mother stirring. "You okay, Mom?"

"Yeah, got my business done. I'll be there shortly."

Peggy Sue heard the toilet flush. *At least, her plumbing's working today. Seems like she either can't go or has to go all the time. Sure hope she doesn't get another UTI. That was no fun. I never knew it could cause hallucinations in women.* "It will be ready when you are, Mom."

Peggy Sue got two coffee cups, one for Mom, which she filled with coffee, and one for her, which she topped with her favorite, Pepsi. She sat at the table, lit a cigarette, inhaled deeply, and then blew it out through her nose. *As long as they keep making Pepsi and Virginia Slims, I can handle anything.*

Her mother hobbled into the kitchen, took her usual seat, sipped at her coffee, smiled at Peggy Sue, and said, "Aw, the world is good. Let's eat."

"Coming right up, Mom." She used the spatula to cut the omelet and placed it on the plates along with the toast. "Here you go, Mom. Breakfast fit for a king, or a queen like you, Mom."

"Why, Peggy Sue. You surprised me. I haven't had an omelet for years, and cinnamon toast. This is wonderful. Today's starting out very interesting."

Peggy Sue smiled. "Yeah, I have a feeling it's gonna be a memorable day. Don't forget your pills, Mom. You did yesterday."

"Did I?"

"You did."

"I don't remember. Funny how I can remember things that happened on the farm when I was growing up, but I can't remember what happened yesterday. Let's not forget to say Grace."

"Sure, Mom."

After Mom said a quick prayer, they ate heartily.

"That was good, Peggy Sue. Could we have this more often?"

"Sure thing, Mom. I'll take care of the cleanup. Need any help getting to your chair in the living room?"

"I think I can make it." She got up and started to walk away. "Peggy Sue, are you doing anything special today?"

"I'm thinking of going out for a little while this morning, Mom, but I shouldn't be long if I do go."

"Get me another romance novel if you would. You know the authors I like."

"Sure thing, Mom." Peggy Sue smiled. *Poor Mom, she's been reading the same novels over and over again and doesn't remember.* "I won't forget."

"Thank you."

Mom slowly left the kitchen, and Peggy Sue cleaned the table and did the dishes. She finished her cigarette and Pepsi and went to check on her mother. She was already asleep in her chair. Peggy Sue placed a blanket on her. Then she got a cup of water and a romance novel and put them on the side table. She sighed. "Poor woman. I don't ever want to grow old and be like that." She listened to her mother's labored breathing before walking to her room.

Yes, today was going to be different. The usual plain blouse, khakis, and loafers wouldn't do. She opened one of the lower dresser drawers and pulled out a pair of men's work blue jeans and a dark men's shirt. In the closet was a men's brown leather jacket. She took it off the hanger and laid it on the bed with the other clothing. Then she pulled the long nightdress over her head and stood naked in front of the mirror. She grimaced as she looked at her body with its large scars. The two across her chest were from the double mastectomy. Her mother looked the same. Breast cancer seemed to run in the family.

The long scar on her lower belly was from a hysterectomy. Her monthly cycle had always been a time of dread with the debilitating cramps that lasted for at least a day or more. She didn't miss those, but the thought of not being able to have children depressed her. She'd always hoped the right man would come along and sweep her off her feet. Then they'd make lots of babies and live happily ever after. What man would want her now?

She looked upward and said, "Lord, I know life ain't fair, and we live in a fallen world. I always wanted to go to heaven, but I was hoping You wouldn't take me one piece at a time."

Johnny Cash's song about the auto worker who took car pieces over the years and built a vehicle out of them came to mind. It ran, but it was a mess. She spoke to the mirror, "Yeah, you're a mess, too, but you're still running."

The image in the mirror seemed to nod and say, "You go, girl."

She smiled and became self-conscious of her nakedness. From a drawer, she got some panties lying next to her mastectomy bras, put the panties on, and then the men's clothing from the bed. She wrapped a towel around her waist to give her a manly beer belly. From the closet, she got some cowboy boots, much too big for her, and put them on.

Then she went into the bathroom, colored her hair with some paint she'd purchased at a costume shop, and rubbed some adhesive on her face. She went back to the bedroom and reached for a Styrofoam mannequin's head in the closet. A fake beard was pinned on it, and a cowboy hat rode on top. She put the beard on her face very carefully and next placed the hat on her head. Large sunglasses came next to cover her face, followed by thin workman's leather gloves for her hands.

Peggy Sue wrote a note on a piece of paper and put it in the shirt pocket. She tiptoed down the hallway and spied her mother still sleeping in the chair. She walked out the side door and got into her car. She had a bank to rob.

Chapter 4

Fall 1967

"Are you sure you want to do this, Peggy Sue? Are you sure you want to quit school?"

"Yeah, I do, Jean. I've thought about this for some time. I hate this place. I'm just putting in my time here, and I don't have to be here if I don't want to be. It's not like I'm an inmate in prison. I can leave anytime I want. I'm sixteen, and the law says I can anytime I want to. I hate this place. What's keeping me here? There's so much I want to do, and I can't if I'm stuck in Cocoa. I know how George Bailey in *It's a Wonderful Life* felt. Jimmy Stewart did a great job portraying him. So it's goodbye, Cocoa. Goodbye, high school building. Goodbye, Travis Hardware Store. Goodbye, water tower. I'm outta here. Jean, I can drive, and I got a car from working my tail off for years at Mrs. Miller's store. You know I'm not afraid of hard work, and if you can work for her, you can work for anyone. I can make it out there."

Jean looked enough like Peggy Sue to be her sister though she was a little shorter. Often the other students and teachers at school mistook one for the other. She thought for a moment and said, "But what about Mrs. Patterson? Who's she gonna find to fill your spot on the basketball team? You know there's no one in this school who can handle the ball like you do, except for Bill, and he's a boy. I think they'll notice if he takes your place on the girls' basketball team."

"Yeah, I thought about that. Coach won't be happy. And yeah, I think they'll notice if Bill takes my place, but he does have nice legs."

The girls giggled, and who would walk by at that time? Bill. They suppressed their giggle though he gave them a funny look as he walked by. He rounded the corner, and they giggled some more.

"You gonna do this, too, Jean? We talked about it. Are you still in?"

"I'm thinkin' about it. I'm leaning that way. That's as good an answer I can give you, Peggy Sue."

"I know. It's a big step. There's so much I want to do right now." She paused. "I'll go talk to her right now. She should be in her office in the gym."

"Coach Patterson's always had an open ear and will give you good advice."

"You're right about that, Jean. I'm going now. I'll see you later and give you all the details of what we said."

"Okay, Peggy Sue. See you then. Bye."

"Bye."

Peggy Sue walked down the hall, turned left again, and went through a double door into the gym. She looked across the basketball court and saw Coach Patterson sitting in her office. She walked around the perimeter of the court, went to the office, and knocked on the window. Coach looked up from her paperwork and gave a questioning look. Peggy Sue mouthed that she wanted to talk with her. Coach tilted her head to say, come on in, which the young girl did.

"Hey, Peggy Sue. What's on your mind today? How's my star playmaker?"

"I'm okay. I got something I need to talk with you about today. I want to quit school. I'm tired of this place. I want out."

Coach Patterson's face dropped. "But why? What's wrong? You got some problems you need me to help you work out? Why do you want to quit?"

"Because I can, and there ain't nothing you or anyone else can do about it. I want to be free to get on with my life right now, and this place is holding me back."

"Have you talked about this with your mom?"

"She don't like the idea, but according to the law, I can do it anytime I want to."

"True, but you really need to get your diploma. You'll need it to get ahead. Most employers want you to have one."

"Coach, I know that, but I can get my GED in a couple of years. Why waste time at school when I can have my freedom right now?"

"I wish you'd stay. What about the basketball team? You're the link pin that holds it together. We'd be lost without you. There's no one in this school who can fill your shoes on the team."

Peggy Sue said, "What about Bill?"

Coach frowned. "Bill's a boy."

"Just kidding, Coach, trying to get your goat."

"You did on that. Peggy Sue, I'm not sure what I can tell you to make you want to stay. The team needs you. I hope you'll reconsider your decision. You know it might be different if we had scholarships for girl's athletics' like we do the boys. Maybe someday we will, but us girls still have progress to make."

"Ain't fair, Coach, that it's boys only."

"I know. It's not fair. Peggy Sue, you'd have colleges begging you to attend."

"Ain't no way I could ever afford it any other way. Mom barely makes enough to keep a roof over our head and food on the table."

"I wish I knew of another way to talk you into staying in school and continuing your education. Please reconsider it if you would. The team needs you."

Peggy Sue sat silently for a few moments as she thought about the coach's words. Coach went back to her paperwork. "Okay," said Peggy Sue.

Coach looked up. "Okay? Okay, what?"

"I'll stay for you and the team, but I'm only committing till the end of the semester when basketball season's over. After that, I'll leave if I still want to."

Coach sighed, "I guess small victories are better than none. I'm glad you're staying for the season, but I think it would be in your best interest to continue with your schooling."

"I'll think about it, Coach. I couldn't see me letting the team down. I could see their faces all down and disappointed. I couldn't do that."

"Thank you, Peggy Sue. You won't regret your decision."

"Got to go, Coach. Class is startin' in five minutes, and I need a pit stop before I get there."

"Okay."

Peggy Sue got up and turned toward the exit.

"And Peggy…"

"What, Coach?"

"If you ever need to talk, you know where to come."

Peggy Sue smiled. "Thanks, Coach."

She walked across the gym and out the double doors and found Jean waiting for her.

"How did it go?" Jean asked.

"She talked me into staying."

"I thought she would."

"But only till the end of the semester."

Jean said, "I want to hear it all."

"Later," Peggy Sue said as she hurried into the nearby restroom, leaving Jean standing with her mouth open. "I need some time to think."

Chapter 5

"I can't believe we're actually doing this, Peggy Sue."

"I told you we could do it, Jean. We've made it this far. We'll make it the rest of the way."

"I guess so. Glad we had relatives along the way."

"Yeah, a place to lay your head and a meal. By the way, Jean, you snore."

Jean laughed. "Ain't that a hoot? You sawed a cord of wood last night, too."

Peggy Sue said, "Sorry about that. I can do that when my nose gets congested. I guess my schnoz doesn't like something out there."

"Where are we now?"

"That small town we just left was Clear Lake. That was where Buddy Holly played his last gig before he died, at the Surf Ballroom, remember?"

"Maybe if someone wrote a song about me, Peggy Sue, I'd remember better."

"Sure, you would."

"Ain't nothin' in Iowa but flat land carved up in big rectangle plots covered in corn or wheat, and whatever that other stuff is."

"Think it's soybeans. Yeah, Jean, it's sure flat like Florida, but it don't look the same. It's monotonous to me. I guess the locals would have a different opinion, but that's how I see it."

"Did Buddy really write that song about you, Peggy Sue?"

"I'd like to think so, but I really doubt it. I like to think my parents liked the song and gave me the name because of it, but I'll never know. Dad's dead, and when I asked Mom about it, she got this far off look in her eyes and never answered. It seemed to trigger a sad memory for her, and I never asked again. So, that leaves me to speculate on it. Anyway, I claimed it as my song, and that's why we're in the middle of nowhere somewhere in flyover country in Podunk, Iowa."

Jean said, "Thought you said the name of that town was Clear Lake."

Peggy Sue laughed, "Jean, are you that naïve? Podunk is an expression for a place dreary and remote not hardly worth putting on a map."

"Oh. So if it was that bad, why was he playing a gig here?"

"Musicians have to play wherever they can find a place, and often someone else is doing their booking, which is one of the contributing factors as to why he died."

"Then tell me the story, Peggy Sue."

"It was the middle of winter, which was why his tour was called the 'Winter Dance Party.' And whoever did the bookings hadn't considered the weather or the long distances between the gigs. It started in Milwaukee, Wisconsin on January 23rd, 1959. The old unheated tour bus, more of a retired school bus, broke down twice, and the band's drummer, Carl Bunch, got his toes frostbitten, so Buddy was looking for other transportation, more reliable and comfortable, to the next show. He chartered a four-passenger Beechcraft to take himself, Waylon Jennings, and his guitarist, Tommy Allsup, to the next venue in Moorhead, Minnesota. It would give them some time for some much-needed rest.

"Waylon Jennings gave up his seat on the plane voluntarily to J.P. Richardson, better known as The Big Bopper. He'd been sick with the flu and said a plane ride would be far more comfortable for a man of his size."

Jean said, "So, The Big Bopper was a large fat guy?"

"He was five foot ten inches tall and weighed around three hundred pounds."

"No wonder he wanted to be on that plane and not the cramped school bus. But wasn't the other musician killed named Ritchie something, not that Tommy guy?"

27

"You're correct. Those guys flipped a coin to see who got the seat, and Ritchie Valens won the toss and died shortly after the plane left the ground and crashed. He was only seventeen."

"Wow, talk about bad luck," Jean said.

"Yeah, and bad planning. The pilot he hired wasn't qualified to fly in the nasty weather they had that day, either. They think that's the main reason the plane crashed." She paused, "Jean, you never know what the fates have in store for us. Got to live every day like it could be your last. That's why I wanted to do this now. School was so stifling. There's just too much to do in life, and I felt like I was wasting it in school."

Jean said, "So here we are in the middle of nowhere, Iowa looking for adventure and chasing our rainbow."

Peggy Sue smiled, "Something like that. Hey, we're almost there."

She slowed down and took a right on a well-traveled dirt road. It had ice-covered potholes that crunched as the car drove through them. At a wide spot in the road where many had pulled over before, Peggy Sue stopped. "This is the place. Somewhere over in that cornfield, their plane went down, killing all four on board. That's where the music died."

Jean was silent for a moment. "It ain't fair."

"No, it isn't. Life's not fair. You got to deal with it, make the best of it, and maybe even twist the nose of fate to make him see it your way."

"I guess so, Peggy Sue. Are we getting out?"

"Yeah, we came all this way, and I want to leave something."

As the girls opened the doors, the harsh Iowa winter winds hit them, and they gasped.

"Wow, colder than a witch's tit," Peggy Sue said.

Jean laughed, "You sure know how to break the ice."

Peggy Sue laughed too, and they hurried over to the makeshift memorial, a cross with wilted flowers around it and the singer's name on it. "I brought somethings I thought Buddy would like."

"What's you got?"

Peggy Sue pulled some plastic flowers out of her coat pocket. "These won't die and turn brown." Then she drew some black-rimmed glasses from her vest pocket. She opened the earpieces, placed them on the horizontal part, and then pulled them closed behind around the upright wooden piece. "There," she said, satisfied. "And one last thing." She placed a guitar pick on the very top of the cross. "What do you think, Jean?"

"I think Buddy would like it."

"I do, too."

The young women stood silently and looked around, trying to imagine what the crash must have looked like. Peggy Sue imagined tangled wreckage and the smell of leaking aviation fuel. Jean spoke, "I'm getting cold. You ready to go yet?"

"Give me another minute, Jean. You go back to the car if you want."

"I think I will."

She walked back to the car and got in, leaving Peggy Sue contemplating. *So this is the place. This is where the music died. Well, Buddy, like you, I got places to go and sights to see before I die. Hope it's not soon, but you never know. Gotta live till you die.*

Peggy Sue thought she heard singing, but it was probably just the wind whispering in her ear. "Peggy Sue, Peggy Sue, Pretty, Pretty, Peggy Sue, I love you, gal, and I need you, Peggy Sue."

She said a little prayer and then walked to the shelter of the car. It started right up, and they drove off. Places to go. Sights to see. The future beckoned for Jean and pretty, pretty Peggy Sue, my Peggy Sue, though right now she felt a little blue.

Chapter 6

After hearing of a coming snowstorm, Peggy Sue and Jean decided to drop south to Missouri and pick up Route 66 and miss the bad weather. The Oklahoma hills were pretty, but the travelers soon grew tired of the flatlands of the state. The wind sure did come sweeping down the plains just like the song said. Panhandle Texas was no better, nor eastern New Mexico. The mountains of the central part of the state were a welcome sight.

"Where are we now, Peggy Sue?"

"We're approaching Albuquerque."

"Alba-what?"

"Albuquerque."

"Are you making that up, Peggy Sue?"

"No, Jean. That's the name of the town. I think it's named after some old Spaniard."

"Those old Spaniards sure got around. Thought they were only in Florida, you know, like St. Augustine."

"Jean, didn't you pay attention in Mr. Dye's history classes?"

"Not really. Why should I? It's just about a bunch of dead people. Who cares?"

"'Tsk, 'tsk. Jean, sometimes you worry me. History's important. Why study history? History made us who we are today. Those dead people were just like you and me. Maybe we could learn something from their successes and failures, so we don't have to make the same mistakes over and over again."

"You sound like Mr. Dye."

Peggy Sue laughed. "You think about it." She pointed to an upcoming sign. "See? A L B U Q U E R Q U E, Albuquerque."

Jean said, "Well, I'll be. I thought you were kidding me, but it's still a funny name. Hey, look at that billboard." It read, In Concert, **The Doors** *featuring Jim Morrison,* El Rey Theater, Albuquerque, NM, and a date below.

"That's tonight. Jean, Jim's from Melbourne, Florida. He's my favorite. Wanna go?"

Jean's eyes grew wide, and she and Peggy Sue screamed like teenage girls and jumped up and down on their car seats.

Jean said, "Let's do it. Wonder if they still got tickets?"

"Only one way to find out. I think the sign said the theatre was on Route 66. Let's follow it, and we should run right by it. Hungry?"

"Yeah, let's stop at a restaurant soon."

Peggy Sue asked, "How about that place?" She pointed to Blake's Lotaburgers. The Blake's sign was held by a smiling man in a red and white striped jacket, a blue top hat, and supported by two blue iron pipes that served as his legs.

"Sure, why not? We're looking for adventure, so why not sample some of the local foods."

"Why not?"

They pulled into the parking lot, found an empty place, which wasn't easy, got out, went into the small building, and waited in a line that moved fairly quickly. They ordered burgers, fries, and cokes. They were taken back when the person behind the counter asked if they wanted chiles on their burgers. They said why not, and then he asked, red or green. They shrugged their shoulders and decided on one with red and one with green. They'd cut their burgers in half and try each.

Their order was called. They picked it up, found an empty seat near the windows, and sat down. The food was cooked just right, and both agreed they liked the burger with chiles, but the green was best. They made a quick pit stop and were soon back on Route 66 going west through downtown Albuquerque.

"There it is!" shouted Jean. "There's the theatre!"

Peggy Sue found an open parking spot, and they walked back to the theatre. Yes, they had tickets, and with a little sweet talking and flirting with the young man selling tickets, were able to get seats up close. There had just been a cancellation. The girls snapped up the tickets, thanked the young man, and flirted a little more, especially Jean.

When they got back in the car, Peggy Sue said, "Jean, you shouldn't flirt so much."

"Got us what we wanted, didn't it?"

"True, but it could get us in trouble."

"Let me worry about that."

Peggy Sue did not respond, and they drove on in silence for a few blocks.

"Look," said Peggy Sue. "Turquoise Museum. I love turquoise. Let's stop."

"Okay, why not? We're on an adventure." Jean smiled.

The museum was in a strip mall. A thrift store was next door. The man at the reception desk told them tours were at 10, 1, and 3. They decided to wait an hour and bought tickets for ten. To kill time, they went next door to the thrift store and looked around. It had the typical stuff you find at a place like that, used clothing, kitchenware, knickknacks, records, and books. Peggy Sue found a leaping dolphin carved from a piece of turquoise she liked, but found the asking price of $20 too steep and passed on it.

At 10 o'clock, they went next door and were given an introduction to all things turquoise. As it turned out, the museum owners were the people who had literally written the book on all things about the subject and had been doing it for three generations. Peggy Sue mentioned the leaping dolphin and the price to the owner. He looked surprised. "At that price, I'd buy it in a heartbeat. Even sight unseen, I know it's worth more than that. If you want it, get it before somcone else, who sees its value, gets it."

After the wonderful and informative presentation, the girls left the museum and went next door. Peggy Sue bought the item, and she was happy she did.

"That's a nice piece," Jean said.

"I always liked dolphins. It's beautiful. I'm glad he told me I should buy it. Twenty dollars seems like a lot of money."

"It is, but if you want something bad enough, you'll pay the price to get it."

"Yeah, life is like that." Peggy Sue looked around. "We can't be more than a half-mile away from the theatre, and there's several motels in this neighborhood. Let's get one for the night and see what else we can get into today before the concert."

"Sounds good. What else did you buy?"

"A book about Butch Cassidy and the Sundance Kid by William Goldman. It looks brand new, but they only charged me a quarter. I always like the stories of outlaws who robbed banks and never hurt anyone."

"You worry me, Peggy Sue."

"Ditto. Guess we're birds of a feather."

They laughed. They walked to the first mom and pop's place they saw and liked it. The old motel was clean, close to the theatre, reasonably priced and had a laundry room to wash their clothes. They settled into their room, and Jean took the clothes to be washed. Peggy Sue got a quick shower, dressed, plopped herself down in an overstuffed chair, and began to read her new book.

Jean came back, also took a shower, dressed, and lay down on the bed. "Think I'll take a quick nap," she said. "Your book any good?"

Peggy Sue nodded, "Yeah. The chapters are short. I've only read two. Seems old Butch was of Mormon stock, but his wild streak got the best of him, and that's the path he followed."

"Sounds interesting. You read, but I'm off to dreamland. I want to be fully charged for the concert."

"Okay, you do that, Rip Van Winkle."

Jean smiled and was soon snoring. An hour and a half passed before she awoke. She stretched and said, "Wow, guess I was tired. How's the book?"

"Good. Very interesting. Butch was quite a character and slick, too. He used his brains, not brawns when robbing banks, and he never got caught."

"Really?"

"Sounded like he enjoyed robbing banks. I think I could do that, if I wanted to."

"Peggy Sue, you frighten me sometimes."

Peggy Sue laughed. "Yeah, I frighten myself sometimes. And sometimes you frighten me. Sometimes it frightens me of what people are capable of."

Both girls laughed. Jean turned on the TV. Jeopardy was on, and they competed to see who could do the best. It was pretty much a draw. They watched another game show, The Price is Right, and Peggy Sue did better at guessing the prices.

"I'm hungry," said Jean.

"Me, too. Let's walk to the grocery store and get some sandwich stuff."

"Alrighty."

It wasn't far to the store. They bought just enough sliced lunch meat for sandwiches now and some later before they went to the concert. Bottles of coke and potato chips completed their meals. After eating, Peggy Sue took a nap, and Jean read the book on Butch and Sundance. Sometime later, she woke with a start. "What was that?" Peggy Sue yelled.

Wide-eyed Jean said, "Either gunfire or a car backfired. Whatever it was, it was close."

"Why's it dark in here?"

"The light went out when the noise happened."

Peggy Sue said, "You look and see what happened."

Jean shook her head. "No, you look. Could be dangerous."

"Chicken."

"Chicken yourself. I'm not getting shot."

About that time, they heard male voices outside. "What was it, Charlie?"

"Transformer blew. Wonder how long it will take Albuquerque Power to get over here and fix it?"

"Could be hours."

"They're not known for promptness."

"No, they're not. I'll call it in, and in the meantime, we wait. Looks like it's just affecting the immediate area. Looks like downtown and most of Old Town aren't affected. Guess I won't be watching TV anymore till the power's back on."

"Nope, guess not."

The girls heard footsteps as the men walked away, and their conversation became garbled.

"Sure glad it wasn't gunshots," said Jean.

"Me, too. The hotel manager said this was an iffy neighborhood, and we should travel in pairs, remember?"

"Yeah, I remember. And watch for that pack of wild dogs. Don't want to end up like that homeless man."

Peggy said, "Yes, that was horrible. Enough bad thoughts, Jean. Let's make some more sandwiches and then head for the concert. I know we'll be early, but they may have a warm-up band before the main event."

"Sounds good," said Jean.

After their meal, they walked to the theatre and were surprised to find it half full already. The usher handed out a brochure that told of local bands who'd play before the main event, The Doors. Some of the bands were good. Some were bad, and one was so bad, they were booed off the stage. The girls felt sorry for them but were glad they left early.

Finally, The Doors took the stage, and what a high energy event it was. Jim Morrison dominated the raised area with his movements and booming voice. He sang "Love Me Two Times," as he gyrated around the stage.

"Light My Fire" nearly brought the house down. Peggy Sue was amazed she could hear his voice over all the girls screaming and shouting. "Strange Days," "Take It As It Comes," "Back Door Man," and other songs throbbed and pounded from the band.

They left the stage after playing nonstop adrenaline-driven music for well over an hour, but the crowd wanted more. For an encore, the band did "Break On Through To The Other Side." The building rocked as the crowd pulsated to the electrifying beat. The crowd screamed for more, but the show was over. The roadies began to clear the stage, and the public started to drift out of the building now filled with marijuana smoke. The girls walked the short distance to their motel, slept well and late.

As they were looking for adventure on their trip, they stopped at Acoma Indian Reservation and saw the old village on the mesa, the giant Indian Flea Market at Gallup, the Painted Desert and Petrified Forest, and stayed in a motel with teepees made of concrete in Holbrook, Arizona. The owners invited them to church the next day and to the picnic afterward. No need to bring anything but a healthy appetite. The girls agreed and met some kind and hospitable people at the gathering.

The next morning they set off again. Their destination of San Francisco was getting closer but stops in Las Vegas, Death Valley, and several other national parks in California would happen. After all, they were looking for adventure.

Chapter 7

The girls were fortunate they found an efficiency apartment in San Francisco they could share. Rent was higher than they liked, but it was San Francisco, after all. Lots of people in a crowded area with no room to expand; what did you expect? Both found jobs as clerks at different hotels, so they had enough to make ends meet but barely. Life was meant to be lived for the moment, and the worries of life seemed far away, well, mostly. The homeless were everywhere, and the city fathers seemed to be clueless about fixing the problem or didn't care. She thought it more the latter. Peggy Sue often gave dollar bills away to them.

"Peggy Sue, you shouldn't do that. They'll just buy cheap wine with it and get drunk."

"Yeah, they may, Jean, but they may get some food with it, too. But then they may get a bottle of wine and drink it all. Maybe it will ease their pain. If I was in their shoes, I'd hope someone tried to help me, even if it was misguided."

Jean shook her head. "There are times I worry about you. Sometimes I think you're too goodhearted for your own good."

"Could be," Peggy Sue said and then smiled, "but that's me, and I won't change."

"Yup, that's the Peggy Sue I know, and if she ever changed, it'd probably kill me with a heart attack."

"That's right. We got the world by the tail. We're free, pretty, young, and adventurous."

"Yuppers, Jean. Maybe even a little reckless and wild."

"Boys ain't the only ones who get to sow wild oats."

"Just remember, Jean, we're girls, and we have to be more careful."

Jean rolled her eyes, stopped dead on the sidewalk, threw her hands skyward, and shouted, "Hey, World, Peggy Sue just had a revelation, 'We're girls, and we need to be more careful,'" but no one paid her any mind. The people just kept walking by like they'd seen it all before.

Peggy Sue grabbed her by the arm. "Come on before someone thinks you're crazy and hauls you away to the loony bin."

Arm and arm, they walked away. Jean said, "In this town, no one's normal. I think they lock up the sane people for their own safety."

"Wish they'd lock up their politicians. They're even more crooked than Florida. At least back home, they did the bulk of their bad deeds in private. Here, they do it openly in plain view, and no one here seems to care or notice."

"True. Peggy Sue, don't go all cerebral on me. We ain't gonna fix something that's been goin' on for thousands of years. Let's have some fun. How far is it to that bookstore?"

"About two blocks. Just around the corner."

They went around the corner, and a stiff wind cut at their clothing. They hurried the rest of the way to the City Lights bookstore and went into the warmth. A speaker was being introduced, and the audience applauded.

Peggy Sue said, "That's Ferlinghetti, the famous Beat poet."

Jean's eyes questioned, who?

"Trust me. He's what's happenin'. He's groovy. Out of sight."

Puzzled but trusting, Jean took a seat next to Peggy Sue.

The poet began, "Thanks for coming tonight. I'd like to start with one of my most famous works from *A Coney Island of the Mind* called *In Goya*. It's about how people find our modern lifestyle so empty. 'America, a country with freeways fifty lanes wide on a concrete continent spaced with bland billboards illustrating imbecile illusions of happiness. The scene…'"

Jean glanced at Peggy Sue and could see she was mesmerized by the man. Jean laughed to herself. *I can't believe we really ran off to San Francisco, and here I am listening to poems being read by some poetry bigwig.*

Peggy Sue turned to her and whispered, "I told you to be ready for adventure."

Jean smiled. *Wonder what new* adventure *awaits us just around the corner?*

Chapter 8

Six months later

The day started out with Peggy Sue on top of the world, and then things changed. Several months before, she'd met Nick and fell head over heels in love with him. It had been great, all she could have ever asked for. She felt like she was a princess in a fairy tale until reality hit her in the face like a club.

Peggy Sue had gone for a long walk in the city to pick up a small package from a store about a mile from her apartment. In front of a store in that neighborhood, a woman was getting in the driver's seat of a car. Nick's car.

Peggy Sue asked her, "What are you doing getting in that car?"

The woman looked puzzled. "Well, ma'am, it's my husband's. Why do you want to know?"

Peggy Sue's mouth dropped open, and she ran around the corner and began to cry. She was devastated. It was impossible to believe, but she'd been dating a married man. And then when she got back to the apartment, she found Jean in bed with a man going at it. There weren't too many rules around the place, but one was no men for sleepovers. Peggy Sue ripped the covers off the naked couple and kicked the man out as he was. She tossed his clothing and shoes out and locked the door.

She glared at Jean, who had managed to cover herself with a long, oversized T-shirt and baggy sweat pants. "What the hell were you thinking, Jean? You know we don't need to invite trouble in. What's wrong with you?"

"I thought you were gone for the afternoon."

But Peggy Sue had her own shocking interruption this afternoon. "Well, I'm here, and you broke the rules. Who was he anyway? Someone from your new job?"

"He's a bartender at the club. Isn't he a hunk?"

"Jean, you know I told you it was a bad idea to go to work there."

"Being a dancer isn't so bad. The money's great. More than I could imagine."

"Dancer, nothing. Call it what it is. You're a stripper. Those places are nothing but trouble, especially for girls. You're not even of age."

"Peggy Sue, I got a fake ID. Please don't tell them that. I can't afford to lose this opportunity. I can see big bucks. You know I've been able to buy a nice car and got money in the bank."

"Jean, don't you see you're just a piece of meat in the sex industry? They'll use you up, spit you out on the trash heap, and find another girl to use, abuse, and toss out. It's a never-ending cycle." She stopped. "Have they got you making dirty movies yet?"

Jean lowered her eyes and nodded.

"I thought so, Jean. You're not even of legal age for that. What would your mother say?"

"You're not gonna tell 'em, are you?"

Peggy Sue thought for a moment. "No. I won't tell them. This is all on you. Jean, I've had it. I'm going home to Florida. You do what you want. Make your own bed and sleep in it. I've had enough. I'm going home."

"But what about your boyfriend?"

"It's over. We had a falling out, and there's no fixing it. I never want to see Nick again."

"I'm sorry, Peggy Sue. I didn't want it to end like this."

"Me, neither, but it has. Jean, I'll get my stuff packed today and leave in the morning."

"Peggy Sue, I don't want you to go. I want it like it was."

"I do, too, but you know I can't see it happening now."

"Let's not leave angry. Tell you what. I'll take you to that burger place, In-N-Out, you wanted to go to. And then a movie about your favorite outlaw has just come out. It's playing at the Regal. I got time before I have to go to work later. My treat."

Peggy Sue frowned when Jean mentioned work but said, "Okay. For old time's sake. I don't want to leave on a sour note."

"Good."

Jean got adequately dressed, and they had a fine time that afternoon, but somehow, it wasn't the same even if the burgers and fries were good, and the movie was super. Of course, they rooted for Butch and Sundance. They wondered if the story of outlaws ever ended any other way. Was it always going down in a hail of bullets?

Peggy Sue packed up her car that evening. She heard Jean come in in the wee hours and go right to bed. Slightly before first light, Peggy Sue got up and fixed a bowl of corn flakes and milk. She washed the bowl and silverware and put them in the drainer to dry. On a piece of paper, she wrote, "Jean. Distance never separates true friends. Hoping you can make it all work out. A friend always, Peggy Sue."

She folded it, placed it on the table for Jean to find, then grabbed her coat, and headed out the door. The car growled as it came to life. It never had liked the cold breezes coming off the Pacific, just like Peggy Sue. The warmth of Florida would be a welcome change. She needed that. After pulling onto the highway, she was eastbound, no turning back. One adventure was ending; another had begun, she hoped.

Chapter 9

1971

What a year it had been. After Peggy Sue had returned from California, without Jean, she'd lucked out and got a good job as a secretary with a company at Kennedy Space Center. A good word from her brother to one of his friends had helped, too, that and the fact she could type at sixty words a minute with few if any mistakes.

She'd had no desire to go back to school. It was too confining, almost like jail. They'd been after her to get her GED, and since she'd turned eighteen, she'd been working on it. The company provided excellent insurance. She'd missed getting regular physicals for lack of money.

An older lady at work had recommended the gynecologist. She'd been going to him for years and had nothing but praise for him and his skills. This was her second visit to him, and she was worried. He'd done the standard female exam she wanted, referred her to a specialist, and requested some more tests. What had worried her most was how guarded he was on his report, but he couldn't hide the concerned look on his face. Now the tests were back, and she was nervously sitting in his waiting room for a follow-up. She feared the worst and thought she was prepared for it.

Wonder if all these offices look the same? Comfortable, but sterile-looking chairs, old magazines, and some potted plants. She sighed. *What's keeping them?*

She looked through the magazines but found nothing that interested her. A side door opened, and a nurse she recognized as the one who had been the doctor's assistant stepped into the room. She looked around. "Miss Tallman?"

"That's me." Peggy Sue got up.

"Please come with me."

Peggy Sue followed her into the next room, where she took her temperature, weight, and other vitals. All normal. "Wait here. The doctor will be right in. You're lucky to have an early appointment. The waits can get longer as the day goes on if the doctor gets a patient that takes longer or has some special needs," Nurse Betty said.

"I took a half-day off from work. I should be able to go back to work after this?"

"Yes, you should," the nurse said, but the look on her face concerned Peggy Sue. Often body language can conflict with a person's words.

Now, what to do? Peggy Sue saw an old National Geographic magazine and picked it up. *Appalachian*

Endangered Plants, Ancient Mayan Ruins, Hunt for Bigfoot, and Florida Aquifers. The last article looked interesting. She flipped the pages and found it. She read a page and was starting on the second when she heard a knock on the door. "Come in," she said. *Please tell me what you found?*

Dr. Nickles entered, followed by Nurse Betty. They both had unsettled looks on their faces. He held a clipboard with pieces of paperwork in his hand. "Miss Tallman, I have the results of your tests, and it's not good news. It's as I feared and talked with you last time. The mammogram confirmed that there's a lump in your breast. You were correct in your self-diagnostic. I found it, too, with my exam last time. It's in the milk ducts, a commonplace for lumps. I want you to go for a biopsy to determine how we deal with it."

Peggy Sue said, "You mean if it's benign or not."

"Yes. You're correct. The mammogram of the other breast also showed a small lump in the same area. I want a biopsy done on it also for safety sake. You put in your family history report that there's a history of breast cancer in your family."

She nodded, "My dad died from it, and my mom's had a double mastectomy."

The look of concern deepened on his face. He looked at Nurse Betty, "Set up an appointment for this and tell them we need it done yesterday."

Nurse Betty nodded.

He turned back to Peggy Sue. "We have the other results back also. There are problems with the pelvic organs, mainly in the uterus. It would explain some of the difficulties you've been having. Has your mother had a hysterectomy?"

Peggy Sue could feel her eyes moisten. "She has."

He sighed, "There's a strong possibility you'll need one in the very near future. We need some more testing."

"Doctor," she pleaded. "Don't you have any good news?"

"We won't know for sure until we do more testing."

Tears ran down her face, "So, you're telling me I've got a snowball's chance in hell of keeping my breasts and uterus. I want a husband and a family. I'm only half a woman without those."

He looked at his shoes. "We won't know till we do more testing."

"What are my chances, doctor? Give it to me straight, please."

The look on his face said it all, "Not good."

Tears poured from her eyes, and she began to weep. She put her head in her hands and sobbed. The doctor looked helpless and turned to the nurse and nodded to her. She understood, sat next to Peggy Sue, and put her arm around her, but said nothing as Peggy Sue continued to cry.

When she could shed no more tears, Peggy Sue looked at the nurse next to her and said, "Thank you."

Nurse Betty smiled, "We'll get through this somehow."

"That's easy for you to say."

"No, I've walked in your shoes. That's why I work here so that I can help. I know what you're going through."

Peggy Sue hugged the nurse, and the doctor smiled weakly. He got some tissues from a box on the counter and gave them to Peggy Sue. "Thank you," she said.

"Miss Tallman, I know this is incredibly hard for you, but everyone here will do all they can to help you in any way we can. We're here for you. We'll get through this."

Peggy Sue nodded. "Thank you, Doctor. Guess I need to get back to work."

Nurse Betty and Peggy Sue got up.

Nurse Betty said, "I need to give you some information and set up some appointments. I'll give you the info now and call when and where the additional tests will be done."

"Thank you," Peggy Sue said. She walked in a daze as she left the office and went to her car. At US 1, she should have turned right, but she turned left and drove to the beach and didn't remember getting there. The parking lot at Cherie Down Park in Cape Canaveral was fairly empty. She parked, grabbed a towel, and walked to the water that lapped lazily before her. After spreading the towel, she sat down and began to cry. The tears came like a deluge, and her sides shook as she trembled.

When no more tears came, she wiped her face with her blouse sleeve and looked out to sea. She could go for a walk and never come back. It wouldn't take long to end her pain. She pondered the thought. No, there were people that needed her. The doctor was right. Somehow, she'd get through this, and she wasn't going back to work today. She had much to think about.

Chapter 10

1985

Peggy Sue pulled her red Pontiac into the parking lot at Lulu's Boutique in Rockledge next to a car with California tags. Traffic had been heavy on US 1 before she pulled off on Barton Boulevard. The day was mild by Florida standards, so she didn't seek out a spot under a shade tree. She walked into the store. "Hello, Miss Tallman. It's good to see you. You haven't been in the store for a while. Let me know if there is anything I can do to help you."

"Sure will, Lulu. Yeah, it's been a while since I've been in here. I think I can find what I want. You've been so helpful in the past. If I need help, I'll give you a holler."

"Sounds good. Just holler. I'll come and see what you need."

Peggy Sue nodded and walked through the displays of women's clothing as she headed toward the back of the store. A woman with a puffy face looked at her with surprise. "Peggy Sue?"

Peggy Sue stopped. "Do I know you?"

"It's me, Jean."

Peggy Sue looked closely. "I don't think I know you."

"It's me, Jean. We were friends in high school. Don't you remember we went to California together?"

"Jean? Is that really you? You've... changed."

"Yeah, I have." Her eyes dropped down. "I know when we last saw each other, well, we parted on a sour note. Some nasty things were said, mainly by me. I've had a long time to think about that. Peggy Sue, I'm sorry."

"It's such a surprise to see you. I'm shocked."

Jean said, "Yeah, been a lot of water over the dam since those days. A lot of water. Say, could we talk? There's a lot of catching up to do."

Peggy Sue thought about it. She was still a little sore about their unpleasant split, but she wanted to know why Jean was here in Florida and what she'd been up to since their last goodbye. "Okay." She was a little surprised when the words came out of her mouth.

"Good. I noticed a Dunkin' Donuts next door. Let's have coffee and something else. My treat. Sound okay?"

"Okay. Let's go."

They walked to the front of the store. "Leaving so soon?" asked Lulu.

"Going next door for coffee," Peggy Sue said. "I'll be back. You, too, Jean?"

"I'll be back," Jean said.

They left the store and walked next door to the donut shop. They agreed on a large coffee and some donuts, glazed and cinnamon sprinkled. Peggy Sue found a seat, and Jean placed the order. In about a minute, she returned with her purchase. "Here we go. Now, let's do some catching up. A lot has happened in my court. How about you, Peggy Sue?"

"That's an understatement. You want to go first?"

"Okay." Jean took a sip of the dark coffee. "That's good. I always liked their coffee. Now, where to begin?"

"From when I came back to Florida."

Jean sighed. "I'm really sorry about what happened the last time I saw you. I was so wrong, and you were so right. Can you ever forgive me?"

Peggy Sue smiled. "I was never good at holding grudges, but I still want to hear what you've been up to."

"Thank you, Peggy Sue." She looked down before meeting her friend's eyes. "I did a lot of stuff I'm not proud of. I was a dancer at the clubs on the west coast."

"A stripper."

Jean grimaced, "Yeah, I was taking my clothes off for money, and it was big bucks. Those horny guys were so easy to lead on and clean their wallets out. I went through a lot of money with wild living, some I'd like to forget. I was doing drugs, as were almost all of the girls. A guy I knew asked if I wanted to make some more big bucks, and soon I was doing porno."

"But you weren't even of age."

"Fake ID's. The producers got real mad when they found out about it years later and had to pull the movies. I did a bunch legal, too. Wish I hadn't now, but that can't be undone. I have to live with it."

"I'm so sorry, Jean."

"It gets worse. I did some other dumb things and ended up in prison for several years. It was there that I found I had advanced breast cancer. With time off for good behavior and a hurry-up from the California Prison Bureau, I got an early release. I had to have a double mastectomy as soon as it could be arranged. I paid for it with money I had left in the bank from my working days. I no longer wanted to stay in California, so I came home to Brevard County. It took a while to find a doctor here. I hoped my fortunes were changing, but no. It wasn't to be so. The doctor found my cancer had spread, and I'm now doing chemo. That's why I'm so puffy. That's why you had trouble recognizing me. The doctor said I'm making good progress, and they should be able to discontinue it soon. I'll still need monitoring, but I'm beating the odds. How's that for a sordid tale? Now that you've heard it, do you still want to be my friend? Do you still want to know me?"

"Jean, we all got a past. Yes, I still want to know you. You'll always be my friend."

"Thank you, Peggy Sue. You don't know what that means to me. I was afraid you'd throw your coffee at me and stomp off. You're the first and only person I've told this to." She took a sip of coffee and then a bite of the glazed donut. "Care to tell me what you've been up to?"

"In some ways, it's been similar. I found a good job when I got back with good insurance. Breast cancer runs in my family, and I had to have a double mastectomy a year later. So far, I've been cancer-free, but as fate would have it, a hysterectomy soon followed. It was a hard time. I wanted to be a wife and mother, but that was out of the question."

"Peggy Sue, you can still get married."

"True, I've had some boyfriends, but when I told them of my history, they drifted away. I don't think it will ever happen."

"I know the feeling. Are you still working at the same place?" Jean asked.

Peggy Sue shook her head. "No, every few years, NASA puts the operations of the subcontractors up for bids. My company lost out. Often only management changes and the personnel stay the same after the names change, but I got let go. It was a real shock after working there so long. I wasn't the only one let go. Now I'm taking care of my mother. She's in the early stages of dementia and needs someone around full time. I'm drawing unemployment, but that won't last long, and it's not that much anyway. The state's one of the worst for benefits. Not sure what I'm going to do when it runs out. My brother said he'd help us, but he's not exactly made of money either."

"Sounds like we both had some tough times."

"And still going through them," Peggy Sue said.

"True," Jean said. "You said you'd had a mastectomy."

"Double."

"But you look so natural and normal. How do you do that?"

"Thanks," Peggy Sue said. "It's the mastectomy bras that do it. I didn't know what to do till I found Lulu's. She fitted me right up and took care of me."

"What's it like?"

"It's not that complicated but does take a little time to get the right fit and feel. She'll start you out with a normal bra. Only this one has pockets where your tatas would be. The pockets are filled with cups shaped like breasts made of foam, water, or silicon in a plastic bag. Get some prosthetic breasts, a.k.a. falsies, about the same size as you were before the surgery. Each cup size per breast is about a half-pound. I used to feel off-balance without the added weight up front to counter what was on the backside. But you can get any size you want, A's to the sky's the limit."

Jean said, "Think I'd just like to look like the old me."

"I can understand that, but sometimes I like to enhance myself and just watch the men's eyes turn."

"That's the Peggy Sue, I know."

She laughed, "Little do they know."

Jean said, "And little do they need to know."

"That's right. You can get about any style of bra, even strapless if you like. They even make swimsuits for gals like us, but you have to be careful with the latter. Those puppies have been known to pop out in the water, especially the foam ones. I've heard of women reduced to tears when they came out and floated away."

"Yeah, that would be embarrassing."

"You can trust Lulu to make it work for you. I've been going there for years."

Jean said, "Looks like we're done here. Coffee and donuts are gone. Let's go and see what she can do for me. I want to feel good again."

"Okay, but give me your phone number. Where are you staying?"

"I have a little cottage on Merritt Island behind a big house off Tropical Trail. It used to be a mother-in-law place for the owner when he needed it for that. Now he rents it out." She wrote something down on the napkin. "Here it is."

"And here's my information, too," said Peggy Sue.

Jean said, "I can't believe how lucky I was to run into you today. I'm so glad we had this little talk. I needed it."

"Me, too. Let's go get you fitted up and looking all normal."

Jean smiled. "I'll be happy when I quit chemo and lose this weight I gained. I bet we still look a lot alike."

"Yeah, I bet we do. Let's go. Times a wasting."

"Yes, it is, Peggy Sue. We have to keep in touch."

"I will. Let's go."

They dropped the napkins in the trash can and walked the short distance to Lulus. Peggy Sue purchased the new bras she'd come for and, after an hour of fittings, Jean finally found her Goldilocks's moment, not too big, not too small, just right. They left the shop, said their goodbyes, hugged, and went their separate ways.

Peggy Sue thought about what had happened. It felt like old times with Jean, and she wondered where this would go. Would it be the same? No. It would be different, but somehow, she knew it could be better the second time around. She hoped so. She needed a friend and confidant.

Chapter 11

1986

A small car pulled onto the grassy shoulder that lined Canaveral Flats Boulevard in front of Roger's old trailer. K9 rose to her feet, and her ears were erect.

"Looks like we've got company, K9. Did you invite a guest over? I don't remember doing so."

Roger tried to determine if the car was a Honda or a Toyota, but most of it was hidden by the vines that grew on the fence. A tall, lanky man got out of the car, Pastor Phil Nassey.

"Hello, Roger. Permission to come on board."

"You know you're always welcome here, Pastor. Come on down and sit a spell."

The pastor opened the gate and walked to the dwelling. K9 ran out the doggie door and greeted him warmly. "Good girl," he said. "Good girl."

"Careful, Pastor. She may look harmless, but that's just a disguise. She could lick you to death."

"So I see." He opened the screen door of the porch. Roger lay reclined in his La-Z-Boy chair, and he had papers scattered all over him and the table next to him. "Roger, am I interrupting something important? I could leave and come back later."

"Well, it is important, but not so important I can't put it aside and talk with a friend."

Pastor said, "You need a refill on your drink?"

"Please, tea would be good. Get one for yourself, of course."

"Can do." The pastor went into the house and got two teas from the refrigerator. K9 got between his legs as he came down the step, and he nearly tripped.

"You okay, Pastor?" Roger yelled as he leaped up from his chair and spilled the papers everywhere.

The pastor made a remarkable recovery. "Yeah, I was always good on my feet like a cat. I'll be all right." He handed Roger the tea, and they sat down. "Sorry to surprise you. Your papers are everywhere."

"Don't worry about them. The ground caught them, and they're all properly numbered."

"Are they important?"

Roger said, "Yup, straight from the governor's office. It's my newest project. He asked me to look into the bank robberies done by Cowboy Gene. See if I could figure out who the desperado is that's doing them."

"Wow, you're moving up in the world. Before long, you won't remember us, little people."

"Lots of laughs, Pastor. You never know when you'll need friends in low places among the little people."

"Touché, Roger. I deserved that. Any luck so far?"

"No, still looking over the files. Whoever this man is, he's slick and good at what he does. Seems like a professional bank robber, but there're some things about this case that strike me as odd, and I can't put my finger on what exactly it is. Gonna have to think on it some more and see if anything clicks."

"If the governor's got faith in you, I do, too."

Roger said, "Pastor, I'll try not to disappoint him. He needs quick results, and I'm not sure it will happen. The best people in numerous law enforcement agencies have come up empty. Not sure I'll come up with anything new, either."

"Just do your best."

'Hope that's good enough. I've been looking at the photos the bank surveillance has caught of Cowboy Gene. What's your first impression, Mr. former deputy?" Roger handed several eight by eleven faxes to the pastor.

"Hmm, looks pretty normal to me. Average height. Standard cowboy hat, vest, blue jeans, and denim shirt. Beard, sunglasses, and gloves. Looks like something you might see any day in this state. It all looks as I said, pretty normal. Nothing out of the ordinary."

"I'm gonna have to agree with you on that. I was hoping you'd see something odd or different that might help us catch him, Pastor. I'm not seeing anything different. And he looks the same each bank robbery." Roger stopped and switched gears. "What brings you to my neighborhood today, Pastor?"

"I'm out checking on the homebound people of the church. I was just visiting one of your neighbors, the Tallmans. Sad situation. Old Mrs. Tallman's got dementia and going downhill fast. Her husband died years ago, and her young daughter is her caregiver, and she's had health issues of her own."

"Can't say I've met them yet. Seems like every family has family members with problems of some sort or the other."

Pastor said, "That's a fact. The Gospel of John tells us Jesus said that we will have troubles in this world, but fear not, He has overcome the world."

"Good words, Pastor. What else brings you here?"

"I need your help. I had a conversation with an atheist. He questioned the creation story in Genesis, and I wasn't able to give him good answers. I knew you were an atheist before you came over from the dark side and started believing this world had to have a Creator. Can you give me some help?"

"I'll do what I can. Pastor, there's been a number of books written on that topic. You need to look into it and get some. You'll find them helpful."

"Thank you, Roger. Could you give me some examples of why you quit believing evolution was fact?"

"Evidence, Pastor, evidence. There's far more scientific evidence for creation than evolution if you can ever determine what the theory of evolution is."

"Please explain."

"Well, the theory of evolution really depends on who's telling it. Commonly held evolutionary facts are constantly changing as new discoveries are found. This happens often, and little notice is given that yesterday's facts were not facts at all. There's not one theory of evolution, but many, depending upon the holder of the theory opinions, speculations, or guesses, how the observable facts were interpreted to fix his or her own take on what evolution is. Think of a football game where the rules are ever-changing to suit the whims of your opponent."

"Like moving the goal post or nailing Jello on a wall."

"Worse than that, like nailing water on a wall. Your football example, when dealing with them, it's more like not even knowing the size of the field or how many points make a touchdown. They constantly change things at will, and the other team's players can't even agree on the rules of the game they're playing."

"Sounds like a recipe for chaos and confusion."

"Pastor, it is, and you point this out to them, and they tell you that you have the problem."

"Sounds familiar."

Roger said, "Let me give you an example of ever-changing facts for them. Got any caves in Florida?"

"There's a few up in the panhandle and lots of caves filled with water over in the central part of the state. I think those people that cave dive must be nuts, but some people really enjoy it."

"That wouldn't be my cup of tea either, Pastor. Back up north in my home area, there's a commercial cavern. One way the evolutionists have used to determine the age of the earth was the growth of stalactites and stalagmites in caves. This cave was very beautiful, and I used to visit it frequently. My parents first took me there as a little kid, and I can remember the guide telling me the cavern and formations took millions and millions of years to form.

"I remember a sign over the entrance that said the cave was at least 260 million years old, but somehow, the cave began to grow younger. The sign was changed to 7-10 million years, then to 2 million, and then the owners took it down altogether. Stalactites have been observed to grow at the rate of several inches a month, and that's not uncommon."

"Interesting. Please go on, Roger."

"Many evolutionists believe in Uniformitarianism, that is, the world has always been the same, and changes are gradual. That's it in a nutshell. Like the main theory or theories of evolution, it, too, has more twists and turns than a drunken contortionist. There is great evidence of major catastrophic events, like a Noah type flood, that they have a hard time trying to explain away.

"Let me give you an example on a smaller scale. Years ago, the first scientists who suggested the Columbia River Gorge was formed by a colossal flood were laughed at, ridiculed, and scorned. Today, the idea is widely accepted that a lake the size of several Western states broke and carved out the gorge in a relatively short time, not over millions and millions of years. And to top it off, many believe it happened more than once in varying sizes. The deep and rich agricultural land along the Willamette River in Oregon was created by sediment left over from the flood."

"Roger, I've never heard this before."

"Yeah, it's information like this they don't want to get out and end their monopoly on multi-millions in funding from the government. Let me give you one more example, and then I gotta get back to work. I mentioned Oregon, and it triggered some thoughts. In that state's Steen Mountains, scientists have found verified evidence of rapid geomagnetic reversals in lava flows. These planetary magnetic field shifts happened in weeks, not millions of millions of years. Creationist theories expected this and can explain it, while the evolutionists were surprised and even bewildered."

Pastor said, "Why aren't the kids in school hearing this?"

"Follow the money and groupthink. They love monopolies and do everything possible to see that only their position is presented to the public."

"Sad, isn't it?"

"Yup, ignorance is not bliss, Pastor. People rarely think about whether what they believe is true and can withstand questioning. I see so much emptiness in this world, particularly on college campuses and among those that call themselves intellectuals."

The pastor said, "Thinking themselves wise, they became fools."

Roger said, "Yeah, it's no wonder the suicide rate is so high."

"Agreed. I believe God made each of us, and everyone has a purpose. It sure helps you get through the tough times we all have in life. Even though it may be storming around us, the sun is still shining above the clouds."

"Good words, Pastor. You'll have to introduce me to that atheist. He'd be a good one for an intellectual debate. You know the line from the Bible, 'As iron sharpens iron, so one man sharpens the wit of another.' Do you think he'd be open to it?"

"He may be open to talking with you, but I'm not sure he'll be open to really listen to anything you say. He's pretty dogmatic. Between you and me, I've heard the condition called stuck on stupid."

"Pastor, I believe most are. I think they're afraid they could be wrong and don't want to consider any alternative. So much for considering all the information available. It wouldn't be the first time I've seen people disregard, ignore, even ridicule anything that goes against a majority view. I lost my job because I asked the professors at my college to think about things like this, but that's water under the bridge. I think I told you that story already."

"Yes, I believe you have."

"Pastor, I believe true science and religious faith are compatible, and there are highways beyond science that lead to truth."

The pastor contemplated this for a moment and then looked at his watch. "Roger, I'd love to talk with you and learn more on this subject, but duty calls. Got another shut-in to see."

"Okay, I got some work to do here, too."

Pastor Nassey laughed, "Like picking up the papers and putting them back in order?"

"Yup, number one on my list, but before you go, I want to leave you with this thought."

"Lay it on me, Big Dog."

"If a man never asks questions about his religion, he's doing it wrong. And if you think science can answer religious and philosophical questions, he's doing that wrong. If anyone thinks science can answer questions about philosophy and morality and purpose, guess what? That's not science, but religion."

"Good thoughts, Roger."

"Stick with your faith and understanding, Pastor. Evolutionary science gives no meaning to life and questions like who am I? To paraphrase one atheist, 'What is the purpose of the universe? None. What is the meaning of life? The same. History has no meaning or purpose. It's just noise and fury, signifying nothing.' Another said that the meaningless of life forces man to create his own meanings. Some do it with wine, women, and song. I knew a lot of them. But other atheists, like the megalomaniac Hitler, created his meaning in world domination and eliminating anyone who he believed didn't fit in it. Stick with what you know and feel in your heart, Pastor. Stick with what the Good Book says gives life its purpose, and you'll be far better off than that depressing atheist. Christians have more meaning in their little fingers than atheists could ever dream of."

"Sometimes you surprise me, Roger."

"My wife used to say the same thing, but she usually was rolling her eyes then."

The Pastor smiled. "Let's leave it at that and get about our business."

"Sounds like a plan. You have a great day, Pastor."

"Later, gator."

Pastor Nassey got up, walked to his car, and soon disappeared down Canaveral Flats Boulevard, leaving a trail of dust.

"K9, got any idea what he meant by calling me Big Dog?" She looked at him and gave him a doggie smile. "So, that's a good thing, is it? I've been called a lot worse."

It was always good to have a visit from the pastor. Maybe he'd stop in for church on Sunday morning. *Wonder who the Tallmans are and where they live? Close by? Maybe I'll meet them someday.*

Roger had to sort the papers, and that was going to be a job. Unlike what he'd told the pastor, he'd had to number the papers himself, and he was only halfway through reading them when the spill happened. *Wonder what other surprises were in store for today?*

Chapter 12

"Looks like we got company, K9. I think it's Suzy. Wonder what she wants?" Roger said.

K9 got to her feet and barked happily.

"Guess we'll soon find out. Suzy, what's up?" Roger yelled. "What brings you to my humble abode today?"

"Is it okay to come on down? I hear your dog yelping? Will she bite?"

"She seems happy to see you, even eager to see you. About the only person, she doesn't like is Bill Kenney."

Roger heard her laugh. "Bill can rub some people the wrong way, dogs, too."

Roger grumbled under his breath. "That's an understatement." Then he said, "Come on down, long lost cousin of mine. If you see a donkey, he's friendly, too." He looked at K9, "Well, to people of goodwill though, you two only tolerate each other." He paused, "Guess that will have to do for now." He turned to Suzy, "What's keepin' ya?"

"I'll be right there."

She opened and closed the gate, then walked down to the old trailer. "Good to see you, Roger. What have you been up to?"

"Did Bill perhaps mention I have an assignment from someone in state government?"

"No, Bill's been pretty busy lately. I haven't seen much of him, but I've been busy, too."

"Well, come on in. Can I get you anything? Beer? Bottled water? Tea? It's sweetened Southern style. I'm out of unsweetened."

Suzy came on the porch. "The tea would be fine. Never liked the taste of beer."

"Take a seat there." He pointed to a lawn chair. "I'll get the tea."

"Thank you, Roger."

Roger went into the trailer and came back with a beer for himself and a tea for Suzy. "Here you go." He handed it to her.

"Thank you, Roger."

"So, what's on your mind, girl?"

"Several things. An update on your son's rehab, some chitchat, and something else." She looked down.

"Hmm. I see. How's Carlos doin'?"

"He's doing super. He's walking without the crutches, still got a little limp, but if he keeps up this progress, he'll be good as new in a year. It amazes me."

"Pastor Nassey would say it's all those lady prayer warriors down at his church praying for my son. I don't know if it is or not, but I'm not goin' to tell them to stop."

"Whatever it is, it's incredible. You seeing much of him?"

"Not as much as I'd like. His mom has kinda pulled back now things are going better. His medical expenses and rehab bills were covered by her insurance more than we thought they would be. A lot of cops chipped in, too, both here in Brevard and down Miami way where she used to work. Seemed she had a lot more goodwill built up than she ever knew."

Suzy nodded, "She loves that kid and protects him like a mommy grizzly. She can be a bit of a bear at times, too."

"That she can. He's her only living relative. It's no wonder she's so protective. I'd like to be more involved in his life, but it's a difficult situation. We all know I'm the boy's father, but I'm not married to his mother, fact is, I'm not even listed on his birth certificate. I really don't have much of a legal leg to stand on now. It's complicated, and we're feeling our way through this maze one step at a time."

"That was the general feeling I got when dealing with them. Carlos seems like a good kid. He's had to deal with a lot in his young life. He does favor you and asks about you a lot. He knows I'm your cousin and seems to think that gives me special knowledge about you."

Roger said, "That's good to know. I hope we can get this sticky thingy worked out to everyone's satisfaction."

"I do, too, Roger, for everyone's sake. Say, that word, thingy. Is that one of those big educated words you learned at the university?"

Roger laughed, "No, cousin. That was from the old mountain home hardscrabble School of Hard Knocks."

Suzy laughed. "I know that place. Bet there's a few like that in the Sunshine State."

"Yeah, I bet there is. Now, let me tell you what I'm up to. You ain't never gonna believe this, but I've been asked by a high ranking Florida state official, who I'll not name, to look into the case of Cowboy Gene?"

"Who?"

"Cowboy Gene, the bank robber."

"Never heard of him."

"I'll forgive you because you're new to the area. He's a serial bank robber in the area who's been driving the cops of all flavors, local to federal, crazy. They can't catch him. He's been running circles around them."

"So, Roger, why did they ask you of all people?"

"Suzy, I guess the last time we talked was years ago when I was drug kickin' and screamin' to your wedding, so let me fill you in."

"Bill's told me a little but not much, so go ahead."

"I'll try to be brief and just hit the high spots."

Suzy laughed, "You could sure tell some incredible stories I remember from our childhood, cousin."

Roger laughed, too. "That hasn't changed, but I promise to try to make it short, okay?

"Okay, but I'll believe it when I don't hear it."

Roger grunted, "Oh ye of little faith. Here goes, after the rude interruption."

Suzy rolled her eyes, but Roger paid her no mind. He began, "I made it through college with excellent grades, undergrad and grad school, then got my Ph.D. and took a teaching position at a local college. I took every opportunity available to travel and go on archaeological digs anywhere in the wide world and learned a lot, more there than I ever did in class. Some in the local police department heard about me, somehow. I still am not sure exactly how, but I used my skills to solve a crime in the city. Soon they were asking me on a regular basis. As you can figure, results get attention, and other agencies were seeking me out for help.

"After my world up north fell apart, I came here to try to escape my problems, and then a desperate Canaveral

Flats Chief of Police Bill Kenney drafted me to help on a murder case. I got deputized into the city police department to make it official. I helped bring closure to several other cases and crimes, and someone at the state capital in Tallahassee took notice, and so here I am investigating the case of Cowboy Gene, the bank robber. That short enough?"

"Shorter than I expected, Roger. How's it going?"

"I'm still going over the paperwork I've been sent by various law enforcement agencies. The guy's slick, I'll say that. I just have this feeling there's something everyone's missed. I can't put my finger on it, but I'll know it when I see it."

"One of those ah-haw moments?" Suzy asked.

"Sometimes it's like that. It remains to be seen. Say, you're about out of tea. Need another one?"

"Please."

Roger got up and entered the old trailer. He came back with a bottle of tea and a beer. He handed the tea to Suzy.

"Thank you," she said and paused. "Roger, there is something that's bothering me. Today's a painful day. You see, I'm trying to keep a straight face, but inside, my heart is breaking. You see, today's the date my world came crashing down several years ago. Roger, you see, today's the day…" Her voice trailed off, and she began to weep, and then her weeping became almost a wail.

Roger was shocked and dumbfounded. "Suzy, what's wrong?" but she continued to wail. K9 got up and went to her. The dog whimpered with a sound best described as concern and sympathy. Roger sat his beer down, went to her, and put his arm around her. Suzy's head fell on his shoulder, and tears moistened his shirt. He held her tighter as she cried. "It'll be alright, Suzy. It'll be alright," but he had no idea if it would. "It'll be alright," he said again, more to assure himself than her. He had no idea what to do, so he held on while her tears fell like hard, hot summer rain.

Chapter 13

Roger continued to hold on to Suzy as she wept. His shoulder was wet from her tears. He wondered what the matter was. Finally, she sniffed, sighed, looked at Roger, and said, "Today was the day."

"You be okay now, Suzy?"

She nodded her head. "I think so."

Roger took his arm from around her and gave her some space. She wiped her face with her T-shirt. "Today was the day my baby boy was born, stillborn. Today was the day my world really started to fall apart."

"You don't have to tell me more if you don't want to, Suzy."

"I got to tell somebody 'cause it's tearing me up, and you're family. Please, do you have a listening ear?"

"Sure, I'll listen. Seems I've been listening to lots of people's problems lately."

She sniffed again. "Consider yourself blessed because people trust you enough to share their troubles with you. Most people are glad you have the problems, and they don't. Most people don't want to listen."

"Guess I can sympathize with people with problems. I've had some in my life. It's always good to share with others who've been through the fires of life, especially the same types of fires you've been through. No one understands what the horrors of war can do to a man but another soldier who was there sharing the foxhole and trenches and fighting alongside shoulder to shoulder," Roger said.

"Very true. Bill mentioned you'd had some difficulties, but I had heard some of it through the grapevine."

"You can always depend on the grapevine and Blabbermouth Bill. He hasn't tried to put the moves on you, has he? He's got quite the reputation as a ladies' man."

"Roger, he said the same about you. And no, he hasn't. He's been a perfect gentleman with me."

"You want to tell me any more about why you were crying?"

Her face fell. "Yes and no. It pains me to tell it, but you need to know why I broke down like that. You see, me and my husband had been having some difficulties before I found myself pregnant unexpectedly. We had two girls, pretty well grown and soon to be off on their own. He'd always wanted a son to carry on the family name, and then when we found out it was a boy, he wanted to make it work. It was really a surprise. You could have picked me off the floor when the pregnancy test showed positive. I hadn't had my monthly cycle for several months, but that's nothing unusual for a woman going through menopause.

"I went in for a sonogram. The nurse doing it told me I was pregnant with a boy but wanted me to get an appointment with my doctor. She asked me if I had any leaking fluid, and I said no. She told me then to do it ASAP or sooner. From the way she was talking, I knew there could be a problem, and I began to worry.

"The doctor worked me in the next day. What she told me was frightening. The baby was developing, but the necessary amniotic fluid was very low, dangerously low. My doctor advised bed rest, drink lots and lots of fluid, and come in weekly or sooner if I felt I needed to.

"I was monitored every week, but things didn't improve. They could find a heartbeat, but it was faint, so I was hospitalized and given IV fluids. My baby would starve to death if it didn't work. And it didn't. My doctor sat with me and told me there was no hope. We cried together like you just saw me doing. We would just have to wait until there was no more heartbeat and induce labor for a stillborn baby. The little boy I named Michael after God's warrior angel put up a good fight for two full months before he lost his battle."

Tears rolled down her cheeks. Roger grabbed a box of tissues and gave them to her. She pulled out a handful and wiped her eyes and face.

Roger said, "You don't have to tell me anymore."

She sniffed, "No, Roger, I need to get this off my chest. They induced labor at week 25. It took twelve hours of intense labor for him to be born. Our hospital had a special procedure for families that lose their babies. They put a white flower outside the room for the nurses and doctors to know what to expect when entering the room. It gives the family time to spend with the child and say our goodbyes. Later, I was moved out of the labor and delivery floor so I wouldn't have to endure the sounds of struggle and new life.

"We had a funeral. Oh, the irony. On the day we had it, my milk came in. Talk about bad timing. There were many reminders, both emotional and physical, of our empty arms, but we had a wonderful tribute to our son we had for such a short time. I don't know why it happened, but it did. I still don't understand why and may never. I grieve with every mother who's lost a child, but I give thanks for the two girls I still have.

"Within a week of the funeral, my husband moved out. He said he couldn't stand to look at me, and he blamed me for losing his son. The doctors told him it was just one of those things that sometimes happens and could have happened to anyone, but he wouldn't listen. The marriage was over, and I tried to hold everything together while my daughters were there. When they left, I had to leave, too. The empty house I called home carried too many bad memories. I split the money with my soon to be ex-husband and, through a bunch of bad decisions, ended up on your doorstep, broke and desperate. Roger, you were a Godsend, an answer to prayer. I don't know what I'd have done if you hadn't needed someone to help with your son."

The two said nothing for some time. Roger broke the silence. "I didn't know any of that. You never know what's goin' on inside another person. On the outside, you see a happy face you think is real, but inside, that person may be falling apart."

"Yeah, you're so right about that." She hesitated. "How are you doing, Roger? I heard you've been through troubles, too."

Roger looked away and sighed. "I have. Lost my wife and son in an auto accident about the same time my professional world was falling apart also." He took a long draw on his beer. "I came down here to try to escape my troubles. When they came to the surface, which was daily, I'd drink myself into oblivion to ease the pain. That went on for two years before that rascal Bill Kenney twisted my arm and drafted me into helping him. That was the first step of my recovery and moving on.

"Since then, I've quit drinking as much, but I still have relapses occasionally. Suzy, I'm just starting to feel life has a purpose again. I'm needed, and I have something to do."

Suzy said, "I'm seeing a side of my cousin I didn't know existed. I thought you were a big tough guy, hard as nails, and invincible."

Roger laughed, "I may be all of that, but I'm a mess, too. I'm still working through my problems. Say, you finished your tea. Need another?"

"Thank you, no." She glanced at her watch. "Where has the time gone? I have to get moving. I've got to get to work. Roger, thanks for listening to me when I needed a sympathetic ear." She gave him a hug. "Roger, don't give up. There's a reason you're still here. You sure helped me when I needed it today."

Roger grimaced, "Now, Suzy, don't go slobbering all over me again. Once a day is my limit. Glad I could help."

She let go and smiled. "Thanks again for being there when I needed someone." She leaned in and planted a kiss on his cheek.

He grimaced again, this time bigger. "Now, why did you have to do that? Are you trying to ruin my image as a big tough guy?"

"No, but even big tough guys sometimes fall apart, too, and need to know they're appreciated."

Roger smiled, "True. I hope you stop in again. We can talk about old times and do some more catching up."

"I'd like that, Cuz. Gotta go. Duty calls."

"See ya, Suz."

"See you, too, Roger."

The screen door closed behind her as she left, and she walked to her car, got in, waved, and drove off.

Roger waved back. "Well, K9, I sure wasn't expecting that." He finished off his beer and got another, then picked up the papers on Cowboy Gene to read over again. He hoped a reread would expose some hidden nugget he'd missed. He read for about fifteen minutes when a pickup stopped in front of his place. Bill Kenney got out. K9 growled.

"Yup, K9. It's him, our favorite flatfoot. Wonder what he wants? It's been a while since we talked. Hope it's some good news. I better get a couple more beers."

Chapter 14

K9 rose to her feet and growled.

"Yup, K9, it's our favorite flatfoot, Chief of Police Bill Kenney. Now behave yourself and don't bite him. Remember what I told you. Even licking your butt wouldn't get the bad taste out of your mouth."

Roger went into his trailer and got two beers from the refrigerator. K9 was lying down but keeping an eye on the approaching lawman. Bill walked up to the trailer without saying a word and had a glum look on his face. "Hello, Roger. Got a minute?"

"Yeah," a puzzled Roger said. "Why the long face?"

"Not been a good day. I'll take that beer, thank you."

Roger handed Bill the beer. He twisted the top off and tipped it back, chugging about half of it. "Ah, that was good." He tilted it back and drank the rest. "Got another?"

"Sure. You know where they are."

Bill went into the trailer and returned with two beers in his hand, one already open and half drank. He sat down in a chair on the porch. "Not been a good day."

"What's wrong? I don't think I've ever seen you like this, Bill."

"You been listening to any news?"

"No, I've been reading and rereading the papers on my newest assignment, find the bank robber, Cowboy Gene. Suzy stopped over for a talk, too. What's up?"

"Some dirtbag in Palm Bay went nuts and killed six people, two of them city cops, wounded a bunch more people."

A curse slipped from Roger's lips. "That's terrible. What happened?"

Bill sighed, "The guy was mad at the world. Hated everyone and made everyone who came in contact with him miserable. He had a running feud with everyone in the neighborhood where he lived, and he lipped off to some kids. They responded in kind, and he got a rifle and started shooting. They got away, but he shot an innocent kid across the street, shooting hoops in his driveway. Then he drove to a nearby Publix Super Market and shot dead two foreign students from Florida Tech. He tried to get in the store, but the employees managed to keep him out somehow.

"He got in his car and drove across the street to the Winn Dixie. Two city cops arrived, and he killed them both. Then he got in the store and shot more people. More police arrived, and there was a big shootout. He grabbed a woman hostage, fled with her into the women's restroom, and refused to come out. After six hours, he let the hostage go and surrendered. You asked why I looked so down. Now you know."

Roger couldn't believe what he had just heard. "Damn."

"Double damn. It's like a nightmare."

"Did you get in on this, Bill?"

"No, but every cop in the south end of the county did. I was taking some training with the Cocoa city police."

"So, what do you think will happen?"

"You really want to know?"

"Yeah."

Bill said, "He'll plead poverty, get a public defender at taxpayer expense, plead guilty in exchange for life in prison, or get the death penalty after a trial and then die in prison on death row before they can execute him in Old Sparky at Starke up in north Florida. That's what I think will happen. It's not been a great day."

"I hardly know what to say."

"I don't think there's anything you can say to make me feel better right now. Just let me stew and drink your beer, okay?"

"Okay, you are off duty?"

"Thank God," Bill said. "Don't think I can take another day like this."

Roger nodded.

Bill opened another beer, took a sip, and repeated, "Don't want to ever see another day like this."

"That's an understatement," Roger said.

Bill nodded.

The two men were silent for some time. "You said you're doing joint training with the Cocoa cops. What were you doing?"

"Learning about the appropriate use of deadly force. How's that for a timely subject?"

"Very true," Roger said.

"It was part lecture, part role-playing, and part simulated exercise training. Roger, there's a lot of inaccurate feelings and information floating around out there among the public. We need to correct some of it while trying to anticipate how an encounter can be made to look by those with an agenda that doesn't include making law enforcement groups look good. It can be a difficult, no thanks situation."

"Make a mistake, and you could be pushing up daisies."

"Yup," Bill said. "And really quick."

"Tell me some more."

"You ever heard of shoot them in the leg?"

Roger said, "Yeah. Is it practical?"

"Let me back up a minute. If there's any way of de-escalating the situation, try to do it. We love a happy ending, too. Cops want to go home to their family, just like any office or blue-collar worker does. There is crisis intervention training available, and I signed up for it. Also, Roger, if someone tells you they're gonna hurt you, believe them, and do what you need to do to protect yourself.

"Now, you asked about shooting them in the leg. Imagine you got someone charging at you hell-bent on destruction. Now imagine you only have a second or less to react, then you got to get your gun out, aim, and fire. Think you can do all that and get an accurate shot?"

Roger said, "Sounds difficult, maybe impossible."

Bill nodded, "More like the latter. Someone with a knife can cover twenty-one feet in a second and a half. Hope you see him make his move. You may not, which gives you less time to react, and your reaction is always beat by their action. A person with a knife has murder in their heart and soul. If they'll attack a cop, they won't think twice of attacking a civilian, male or female.

"The other number you have to remember is a hundred and eighty feet. Less than three percent of the population can throw an object big enough to seriously hurt you beyond that. Small stuff will give you stitches, but a brick will drop you to your knees. In urban areas, everything's paved, mobs bring everything that's cheap, and they can throw. You name it; it's been thrown at cops. One cop in our group worked in a big city up north before coming here told of a guy that could throw a golf ball almost the length of a football field. A bag of golf balls is around five bucks. You can equip a whole mob for next to nothing.

"A law enforcement official can use deadly force in specific cases, 1- to prevent the escape of someone trying to escape from custody or to effect the arrest of someone he reasonably believes has committed a crime or to defend himself or a third person, 2- to defend himself or a third party from someone threatening them with deathly force. It's a little more complicated than that, but that's the nutshell version.

"Where do you aim? The torso. It's a bigger target, and shots there are more likely to stop them. Why are we trained to take multiple shots? It can take more than one to stop them. Now, imagine you find yourself facing a big man with a knife up close. Your heart is pounding so hard you can hear it in your ears, every sense is on hyper-alert, every nerve you have is on fire, and you can taste fear in your mouth plus acid from your stomach. The subject person may be distraught, erratic, out of control, drunk, out of his mind on drugs, so hopped up it could take six grown men to take down a little guy. You may or may not be dealing with someone acting rational and reasonable. It's like going to war and unless you've walked in a law enforcement officer's shoes, have some understanding and not assume immediately the cop was wrong. There are a few bad cops out there, but a good agency gets rid of them as quickly as possible."

"Bill, I've worked with cops, but a lot of what you just told me was a surprise."

Bill laughed, "It is for most people. One fellow in the class had a scar on his face and nose that looked like a pinball game flipper. That was from a drug dealer. He'd also had to deal with people high on PCP. Often you'll find them naked on roofs. The police force up there had tried everything nonlethal to subdue them with very little success. Nets, poles, ladders, fire extinguishers, blankets, ropes, nothing worked. One big fellow required four men to bend his arms into the handcuffs. Batons were even discussed, but the general consensus was they just make the guy mad. Tear gas is another hot potato. Seemed it got more of us then the bad guys when the wind changed. You want to do the right thing, but your opinions are limited by reality.

"Roger, I'd like to get you into some of our physical training. There's nothing like being attacked by a man built like a football front lineman even if the knife he's carrying is only rubber. You get an idea fast about what you could be up against and how the outcome could go. Sometimes police train with paintball guns to give them an idea on what needs to be done and if you can hit your target. Some of the training gets quite realistic and isn't for those with a weak stomach.

"So that's been my day. Bad news and training to try to prevent bad news." He paused, "So Suzy stopped in to talk. What did you guys talk about?"

"It wasn't about the killings. Guess she hadn't heard, either."

"Well, what was it, Roger? Did you talk about me?"

"Your name did come up. She said some nice things about you. I was surprised."

"Why?"

Roger said, "I expected old Bill to try to take advantage of the situation of having a sweet young thing under the same roof, even though she does have her own private efficiency. She said you'd been the perfect gentleman with her. What's up, Bill? You got a new squeeze you're lovin' on or something?"

"Why Roger, you surprise me and disappoint me, both. FYI, I never mix business and pleasure. Not that's she's not a sweet young thing. I'm not blind. I may be the candidate for glasses soon, but she's not even on my radar as a squeeze."

"Really?"

"Really." Bill paused. "Well, we've talked a couple of times together on my porch. She seems like a nice lady, but seemed to be holding back. Guess when she feels more comfortable with me, she'll share more of her thoughts. Any idea what could be bothering her?"

Roger said, "Bill, it could be her divorce. She got hurt pretty bad by that. Could be a number of things."

Bill looked at Roger suspiciously, "But, I bet you know."

"And I'm not telling you."

"Good call, Roger. Don't break a trust. If and when she feels like talking about it, she will. I won't push the issue, and for the record, this subject, whatever it was, never came up."

"Sounds good to me."

"Let me change the subject. How's your new investigation going?" Bill asked.

"You mean Cowboy Gene."

"Right as rain, Roger. Have you come up with anything new that all the others haven't?"

"Not yet. The investigations done seem quite professional, but they've all come up empty. There's got to be more information available out there somewhere," Roger said.

"Why don't you talk to some of the investigators? You know as well as I do, they can always add something that never made it into the records."

"Bill, we think alike. I got several names. Any idea where I can find the FBI agents or the local investigators?"

"I think I can help you on that. Give me a list of names."

"Sure."

Roger took a sheet of paper, wrote some names on it, and handed it to Bill who looked at it.

Bill said, "Roger, I know some of these guys, some names arc familiar, and some I'm gonna have to check into. Give me a day or two. That be soon enough?"

"That'll work, but no more, and as soon as possible, please. Need another beer?"

"No, I'm good. I've had a little time to unwind. Nice to talk to someone and not have to be careful with what I say. Some of those cops seem to be looking out for number one and would stoop to snitching on you over some nonsensical matter to a higher-up. Glad my chain of command is short."

"Got you there, Bill."

"Guess I better be goin'." He stood up a little rubber legged.

"You okay to drive, Bill?"

"Yeah, I am. Been sitting too long, and my butt fell asleep. I'll be fine."

"Okay, it's your call."

Bill smiled. "Roger, you do have a good listening ear."

"And a goodly supply of beer."

"That, too. That never hurts. Roger, I'll be goin'." He thought for a moment. "Oh, yeah, Suzy's invited me to dinner tonight. Having steak, salad, taters, and something else."

"And I wasn't invited?"

"She's got better taste than that, ole buddy."

Roger snarled, "Huh, I'm glad you're a friend, or I wouldn't take that sitting down, ole buddy."

"Just kidding, ole buddy."

Roger said, "I expect you to continue to be a perfect gentleman with my cousin."

Bill smiled, "You know me, Roger."

"That's why I said what I did. I better not hear you were up to no good."

"You won't."

Roger growled. "You get out of here, ole buddy."

Bill grinned, "Yeah, I'll be late if I don't." He looked at his watch. "Thanks for reminding me."

"Just go and get me those guy's contact information."

"Okay, will do."

Bill walked out of the porch and meandered down the path to the Canaveral Flats Boulevard. He got in his truck and drove off.

"Dog, let's find something for dinner, too. Bet your tummy's feeling empty, too. Wonder if we'll have any more visitors today? Wonder what else is on the horizon? Wonder what Cowboy Gene's up to today? Wonder where he is? No comment, K9? Guess it'll work out."

Chapter 15

Roger pulled into the parking lot at the Merritt Island Sheriff's Department. Water splashed when his tires hit the puddles. The day had started out dark and gloomy and had gotten no better. He turned the truck's lights off. He'd needed them with the thick clouds overhead, and besides, Florida law required them to be on when it was raining.

By habit, he parked under a tree. Usually, a shady spot was desired to keep the vehicle from becoming like an oven inside on a sunny day, but this wasn't a sunny day. Nevertheless, he remained there and turned off the engine. Almost immediately, something hit the truck on the roof. "Squirrels, tree rats, I'm beginning to hate those little varmints," Roger muttered to himself. *At least up north, they're big enough to eat.*

Another something hit the truck, then another, and Roger saw white splats on his windshield. *Birds, not squirrels, birds!* Roger cursed under his breath as the white bird rain continued to fall. He started the truck, threw it in reverse, and nearly hit a car going by. The driver honked the car horn hard and long as he drove by. Roger cursed again. His mood that had matched the weather went from bad to worse. Counting his blessings at not hitting the car, he found another parking spot, not under a tree. He wasn't exactly looking forward to this meeting, but he knew he had to do it. No use in putting it off any longer. He had to have **the talk** with Hernandez, the mother of his child.

He got out of the truck and sprinted to the building through the rain. The secured door buzzed as he neared it. He quickly went in and saw Charlotte, the secretary, sitting at her desk. "Thank you, Charlotte. Standing out in the rain, waiting to be let in, is no fun."

She smiled, "I saw you coming and did you a favor. Not everybody gets it, Roger."

He smiled back, "No. You mean to tell me some people may have to wait out in the rain unnecessarily?"

"Could be depending on their attitude and if they caused grief while they were here, but you never heard that from me."

Roger smiled and winked. "Gotcha. Hernandez in?"

"She's in."

"How's her mood today?"

"About like the weather."

"Thanks for the heads up, Charlotte."

"You're welcome. What's you need to talk with her about?"

Roger said, "It's double top secret."

"I thought so. I'm glad you didn't say, 'I'd tell you, but then I'd have to kill you.'"

"Nope, wouldn't think about it. Too many guns around here. May not end well, Charlotte."

"Lot of wisdom in that statement. Want me to let her know you're coming?"

"Better if you don't," Roger said.

"Whatever you say. Good luck, Roger."

"I'm gonna need it."

Roger went up the steps and found Hernandez's office door open. She was on the phone, talking. After seeing him, she motioned him in, pointed to the coffee, and mouthed, "Give me a minute or two."

He gave her a thumbs-up, got some coffee, then sat down as she continued to talk, something about her service vehicle being in the shop. The call ended. She looked at him and said, "What's on your mind?"

"We need to talk."

"I thought so. About the elephant in the room?"

"Yup."

"Roger, how about we do it over lunch? My dime."

"I can't refuse an offer like that."

She said, "But there is one catch."

"What's that?"

"We take your truck. I don't have any wheels. Damn vehicle's in the shop again."

"No, not broke down again?" Roger said.

"No, routine maintenance this time. Seems like it spends more time in the shop than in service. It is what it is. Not much I can do about it, but go with the flow on this matter."

"It's a deal. When are you ready to go?"

She said, "It's a little early, but yeah, I can go now. I'm hungry, and I'd like to get this matter over."

"Okay," said Roger.

They got up and walked down the stairs with Hernandez in the lead. Roger noticed the rise and fall of her hips. It brought back pleasant memories of their time in Las Vegas. The sex was good, but Roger knew it took more than good sex to make a marriage relationship.

They stopped at the bottom of the steps. Hernandez said to Charlotte, "I'm going to lunch. Let my calls go to the answering machine. You know how to reach me if some emergency comes up."

"Sure thing, boss."

As they walked out the door with Gloria Hernandez first, Roger turned to Charlotte. She winked and mouthed, "Good luck."

Roger gave her a thumbs up.

As they neared the truck, she noticed his white splattered truck and laughed. "Looks like you got the blessings of many birds."

"You could say that. It's a blessing I'd gladly let someone else have."

Gloria said, "Yeah, the folks that work in the building have learned to watch the weather, so they know where to park for their vehicle's well-being."

"That's for sure. I was hoping the rain would wash it off, but it just seems to have smeared it and made it worse. I'll get it off the windshield so I can see. Maybe I'll still get lucky, and the rain will do its job. If not, it's a trip to the car wash."

She nodded. "Sounds like a plan. Could you do it after lunch? All of a sudden, I got even hungrier. Where to? Some place close, okay?"

"Sonny's BBQ?"

"Good choice. Let's go. I feel like I could eat a horse."

Roger said, "No horse meat at Sonny's but about everything else."

She said, "My stomach's growling and if I don't get something soon, I may take a bite of leg of Roger."

Roger smiled. "Down girl."

They got into Roger's truck and were soon on Courtenay Boulevard going south. As they neared the spot where their son, Carlos, had been hit and almost died, Gloria grimaced and said as she crossed her arms, "I hate it every time I drive by here. We could have lost him right then and there."

Roger said, "Yeah, we could have. He's our little miracle. I was so afraid he'd not make it."

"Me, too."

"Want to talk about it now, Gloria?"

"Let's wait until we're at the restaurant and ordered our meals. We can talk for a while then."

"Okay," Roger said. "We've got a lot to talk about."

She nodded. "We do."

Chapter 16

They pulled into Sonny's parking lot, and Roger picked a spot, not under a tree. No point in a chance of a repeat bird performance. The pair raced to the door and went in. A young skinny blonde girl who looked to be about sixteen greeted them. They asked for a spot where they could talk in private. The greeter smiled, "Right this way. Shouldn't be a problem."

They followed her around the corner and found they were the first guests in the restaurant that day. She took them to a remote booth in an out of the way wing of the building. "This be okay?"

They said yes and sat down. She gave them menus, took drink orders, and left. Roger said, "I think I want a sampler. You're talking about being hungry made me hungry."

"That's a good choice, but I think I want a pork sandwich and french fries."

"Remember, Gloria, your treat today."

She smiled. "I remember, and I knew you wouldn't let me forget."

He laughed, "True."

The waitress returned with the drinks. Roger got a beer and Gloria, a large Diet Coke. She took their food orders and left. Neither said anything for a few moments.

Gloria said, "What's you working on now, Roger?"

"Would you believe the governor asked me to look into a case?"

"I'm not surprised. Roger, you're good. What case?"

"Heard of the bank robber, Cowboy Gene?"

"Cowboy Gene," she said. "Who hasn't? How's it going?"

Roger said, "I'm making a little progress, but I can see why he's not been caught. He's a slick character. It's gonna be an uphill battle, for sure."

There was quiet between them for a moment. "Well, Gloria, where do we go from here? What do we do about Carlos? He's our son. You're his mom with custody. I'm not even on his birth certificate, but we all know, including him, that I'm his daddy. What are we gonna do?"

She said nothing for a moment, sighed, and spoke. "You summed it up nicely. What do we do? Roger, I don't know. That's why I've been avoiding you. I don't know. I ran a gazillion scenarios through my mind on what would work, what wouldn't, what was best for you, me, and most of all, Carlos, and I couldn't come up with what would be best. I did see options I didn't like."

"That's a start. What were they, Gloria?"

She looked down and then took a sip of her drink. "Be like a mama grizzly with rabies and fight like mad. Surrender him to you. Or do nothing. Leave things like they are."

"Can't say I like the sound of any of those. None seem fair, but the third's the best of the worst choices."

"Roger, on that we agree. The mama in me wants him all to herself, but a boy needs a dad, especially when one's there that wants to be a part of his life, but I'm not about to turn him over to you."

"Didn't think you'd want to do something that drastic, nor would I want you to. A kid needs a momma and a daddy. I want to be a part of his life."

She thought for a moment. "Maybe I have a step forward. Want to hear it?"

"Most definitely. Shoot."

"He's been asking about you, and it's been driving me nuts to keep putting him off, but there's that problem; you're not on the birth certificate. If you were with him and he got hurt, you could legally do nothing for his welfare. And then there's the other problem; how would it look for an old guy like you to be running around with a young boy?"

Roger nodded, "Gloria, we're on the same track. I've thought about that, too. Seems like I need some legal rights if we are to move forward."

"I know, and it feels like I'm losing a part of me if I do that."

They said nothing for a few moments, and then the waitress came with the food. "Everything okay? Need anything?"

"I'm good. On second thought, I'd like another beer." Roger said.

"I'm good," Gloria said.

The waitress left.

She looked at Roger, then her food, and then back at Roger. "Let's eat. Let me think about it, and I'll give you an answer when we're done."

"Fair enough. Let's eat."

She nodded.

The waitress returned with another beer.

"Thank you," Roger said.

She smiled and walked away.

"My, this sandwich is big. Want some?" Gloria asked.

"Sure."

"I think I can spare about a quarter of it. Interested?"

"Definitely. Those pork sandwiches are to die for."

"To die for? Roger, you sound like a Valley Girl."

"Frightening, isn't it?"

"To die for."

They laughed and dug in. Neither said anything more as they ate. They finished, and Roger downed the last of his drink. "That was good."

"It was," Gloria said. "Roger, I want to thank you for all the help you've given with Carlos. You were there, and that's saying a lot. I don't know how I'd done it without your moral and financial support. Thank you."

"You're welcome. Glad I could be of assistance."

"Think there's any chance of you and me, you know, tying the knot?"

"Nope. I think we'd drive each other crazy pretty quick."

"I think you're right."

Roger said, "I think the sex would be good, but it takes much more than that for a marriage."

She blushed and grinned a little. "Yeah, it was good, but you're right; it takes more than that to make a marriage work." She stopped. "I'll do it."

"Do what?"

"I'll see about listing you as father on his birth certificate. I think that would be a good start."

"Gloria, I do, too. Thank you. After losing my other son, I want another chance to be a father to a child. Thank you."

The waitress appeared with the check. "Here you go. Any dessert?"

"None for me," Roger said.

"Me neither," Gloria said.

The waitress said, "Please come back soon," and left.

Gloria grabbed the check. "I got this."

Roger said, "I'll get the tip."

"Know any good lawyers, Roger? I think I'm going to need one for this."

"Heard that Hedman fellow's good. I'd start with him."

"Thanks, Roger. I've heard that name mentioned around the office, and it was always in a good way. I'll give him a call, probably tomorrow. Today's full. It'll have to be tomorrow."

"That'll work. Let me know how it goes and if you need any help."

"Will do."

Roger left a tip, and Gloria paid the bill as she promised. They chatted little as they rode back to the Sheriff's Department Building. Roger rode up to the front door, and Gloria got out.

"Thank you, Roger. Maybe we can make this work. I think we've made some progress on this matter."

"I do, too. Keep me in the loop, okay?"

"Will do."

She walked around his truck and headed toward the entrance. At that moment, the clouds opened up, and a beam of sunlight shined down on them. She turned to Roger and smiled. "A sign from above, Roger?"

"I'd like to believe so."

She smiled and entered the building.

Roger sat in his truck and thought. *Yup, maybe, just maybe, we can make this work.*

Chapter 17

1984

"Mom, you be okay if I go out for a while?"

"Yeah, Peggy Sue, I'll be alright. You won't be long, will you?"

"No, I shouldn't be long."

"Okay, I'll be here watching some reruns. *I Love Lucy* should be on soon."

"Okay, Mom, I'll be back soon. Bye."

"Bye, Peggy Sue."

She walked out of her mom's little house, got in her car, a 1976 Pontiac Grand Am, and took off. Somewhere, out there, was what she was looking for. She drove around a while and found it, a car in a secluded area where she could do her dirty work, steal the car's license plate. After pulling in next to it, she grabbed two screwdrivers, one a straight and one a Phillips #2, and got out. Quickly, she removed the screws, threw them in the bushes nearby, grabbed the car's plate, and took off in her car. It had taken less than a minute for the deed.

In a few minutes, she was back home. Peggy Sue walked into the house and found her mom asleep in the overstuffed chair. *I Love Lucy* was playing, and it looked like Lucy and Ethyl were working at the chocolate factory. As usual, bedlam reigned. They couldn't wrap the chocolates coming on the conveyer belt fast enough, and the situation was getting desperate for the women. They tried to eat the extras, but there were too many, and all they succeeded in doing was covering their faces in the dark brown chocolate and feeling sick. Next, they tried to drop them down the front of their dresses. Peggy Sue smiled and laughed quietly so not to wake her mom.

Might as well do it now, better than waiting. She went outside and switched the car's plates. Then she went inside and quickly transformed herself into Cowboy Gene. She peeked in on her mom as she tiptoed out. Mom would sleep in that position for at least an hour, more than enough time.

She hopped into the Pontiac and headed to Titusville. After finding a suitable spot to park on a side street, Cowboy Gene walked the short distance to First National Bank of Titusville. It wasn't busy inside. Cowboy Gene liked that. Less chance of something going wrong. He picked a teller and waited in the short line until it was his turn. He walked to the counter, where a very young female teller smiled cheerfully.

115

"Howdy, cowboy," the young woman said, "How can I help you?"

Cowboy Gene handed her a note. "This is a robbery. No marked bills. No dye packs. I want ALL you got."

The teller tried to keep her composure as she handed over a large stack of cash. Cowboy Gene smiled slightly, put the loot in a satchel, walked out of the bank, and then the short way to the getaway car. Someone seemed to be following at a discrete distance, and he thought that person was trying to get the car's license plate number. Cowboy Gene smiled and drove a twisted route down the side streets of the old Indian River City section of Titusville.

After a left on Cheney Boulevard, Cowboy Gene went south on US 1, never going over the speed limit, always staying below it. Several miles later, he found the road to the right he was looking for. A few miles later, he pulled down the long driveway where Peggy Sue and her mother lived, then turned the car with the back to the house and the nose to the main road. Cowboy Gene gently went in the house past the still sleeping older woman, and transformed back into Peggy Sue. The satchel with several thousand dollars in it she placed in the closet. She'd count it later. Peggy Sue walked back outside, removed the stolen plate, and put the proper plate back on her car. She smiled. She'd done it again and got away. If someone did get the tag number and tracked it to the owner, they'd find nothing but another dead end trying to apprehend Cowboy Gene.

She remembered her sleeping mom and went inside. "Peggy Sue, is that you?"

"It is, Mom. Everything okay?"

"It is, but I'm getting hungry. What are you making for lunch?"

"Sandwiches. Egg salad sound good?"

"Yes. Don't forget I like sweet pickle relish on mine."

"Sure, Mom. I won't forget."

"And a piece of lettuce would be nice, too."

"Sure thing. Give me a few minutes. How were your TV shows?"

"Okay, I guess. Think I fell asleep."

As usual. "Glass of milk, too?"

"Please."

Peggy Sue quickly got their lunch ready. With the money hidden in the closet, they'd live okay for the next few months, but it wouldn't last forever. It was time to start looking for another bank to rob. The money sure came in handy, and it was kind of fun and exciting to live on the edge and get away with it. She had to be careful not to get caught. Each time, she got a little better, learned a little bit more in the fine art of bank robbery. If she ever got caught, maybe she'd write a book about it. She thought for a moment. No, she didn't want that information to get out. Someone may get hurt. A little knowledge can be dangerous.

Chapter 18

1986

"Hello, Mr. Pyles. It's good to meet you," the retired FBI agent said. He stuck out his hand to Roger.

"Thank you, Mr. Twigg. I was glad you agreed to meet with me." They shook hands.

"You made it easy to identify you when you said you looked like Sam Elliott. You could pass for his twin."

"Yeah, I've been mistaken for him regularly. Got me in trouble several times."

"I can imagine. You picked a good place to meet. I love this place. We needed a good restaurant in Port St. John."

"Mr. Twigg, I'm new to the area. Only been in here once, but yeah, it was good. And just call me Roger. Mr. Pyles seems so formal."

"Okay, Roger. Call me Virgil."

"Sure thing, Virgil. Let's go inside. The air conditioning will feel good."

"Yeah, it's a hot one today."

Roger opened the door, and they went inside.

"Hey, guys. Welcome to Kelsey's. Take a seat anywhere you can find an open table," the short lady behind the cash register said. She had an accent. Roger thought it could possibly be Greek.

The place was busy, but it was lunchtime. They found a spot by the front window, and a waitress came with menus and took drink orders. Both men wanted water with ice. She left to get that.

"What're you having, Roger?"

"Steak bomb with fries sounds good. You?"

"That number 3 calzone and a mini Greek salad sounds fine."

"It does. I've had it but want something a little lighter. Gotta look after my girlish figure, you know."

Virgil laughed and tugged at his ample tummy. "Doctor's been after me to lose weight, but I'm losing the battle of the bulge. Maybe, I'll start my diet tomorrow, but then again, maybe not." He laughed, as did Roger.

The waitress came and got their order.

"So, Roger. How can I help you catch this Cowboy Gene? We tried for years and got next to nowhere. You told me you had all the papers on this case. What more can I add?"

"As I told you, I got asked by the governor to investigate this case. He was real good about getting me access to papers from various agencies. I think I got most of them. Probably a few more out there I need if I can figure out what they are and where they are. What I would like is for you to tell me anything you feel is important and would help me. I can read the cut and dry information on the case, but there's a feel, you might even call it the taste and smell of the case, I'm looking for. Do you know what I mean?"

"Yeah, Roger, I do. Let me see. Cowboy Gene's robbed a lot of banks across central Florida and always got away scot-free. Always seems to work alone. Never has a lookout or a getaway driver. He's always polite, never really threatening. Never flashes a gun and never seems in a hurry or gets rattled. Seems to know exactly what he's doing. Gets in and out of the bank in less than a minute. Skilled. Efficient. Most of them are lazy, sloppy, unimaginative, haphazard, and therefore, unsuccessful. Cowboy Gene's none of that. Got to say, if you can understand this; I kind of admire him and his abilities. He's one of the best I've ever seen in all my years with the FBI.

"Most bank robbers are amateurs, druggies, and thugs looking for money to feed their habit or themselves. They're usually frightened as hell themselves when they burst in and then scare the hell out of everyone in the bank. Their heads spin around about like a pinwheel in a hurricane, looking for security guards. They twitch, yell threats, wave guns around, grab the loot, run out of the building, and then tear out, leaving wheels spinning and tire smoke billowing everywhere. Cowboy Gene was just the opposite, professional in every way. He was good.

"He was making me and other agents pull our hair out. For me, there wasn't much left to pull out, but Cowboy Gene cost me follicles I couldn't afford to lose. We couldn't figure old, dried-up looking cowpoke could run circles around us, day after day, time after time. It was frustrating but challenging matching wits with a worthy adversary.

"Roger, I put my years in with the agency and decided to take retirement. I can truly say I miss chasing bank robbers the caliber of Cowboy Gene. I envy you."

Roger looked surprised. "Why?"

He leaned forward. "Don't you see? It could make you famous. You've been handed the opportunity and case of a lifetime."

Roger rubbed his chin. "Never thought about that point. Not sure I want to be famous."

Virgil shook his head. "You're not a career man, are you? They'd kill to be the one to find and capture Cowboy Gene. Some would give their left nut to solve this case and get the glory associated with it." He paused. "Maybe you're just the man that can catch him. A lot can get done when you're not worried about who gets the credit, but I warn you this; there're some out there that may get in your way in the hopes of advancing their own success. You may even have some that will try to steal away the credit you deserve and even try to discredit you and your work. They'll see you as a competitor. Keep that in mind and contact me anytime you need to. I'd like to be in the loop if possible. I'm letting you know I want to run alongside you in this race and be an encourager. I want to see Cowboy Gene caught."

"Thanks for the advice. I'll keep that in mind. I figured there'd be some out there who'd not welcome me in this endeavor and even want to see me fail. Thanks for your support." Roger turned his head and saw the waitress coming with their food. "Looks like it's time to eat. Do this for me. While we eat, think about anything additional you'd like to say and any more advice you like to give."

Virgil nodded, "Sounds good to me."

"Here you go, boys. Enjoy. You need anything more, let me know."

"Okay," they both said.

When she was out of hearing, Roger said, "That's a cute little backside she's got a wigglin'."

Virgil says, "It is. Front side's not so bad either, but she's the age of my granddaughter."

"And I could have children her age." Roger shook his head. "Life ain't fair. Time and tide wait for no one."

"You're correct. Now, are we going to talk about our frustrations with the passing of time or eat?"

"Let's eat. That should give us some satisfaction."

"Good point, Roger."

They said no more and chowed down. The food was as good as it smelled and looked. They made some small talk about the great meal and the weather but said nothing about Cowboy Gene. After finishing, Roger said, "That was satisfying. Any last thoughts you'd like to share before we go?"

"Only one, but I have your phone number, so I'll give you a ring if I think of anything more."

"Sure. I got a question. Why is he called Cowboy Gene?"

"Good question, Roger. Some people say he reminds them of Gene Autry, the singing cowboy. Others say it's because of the blue jeans he always wears when he robs the banks. I don't think he looks like Gene Autry, but he got labeled the moniker Cowboy Gene by the newspapers, and it stuck."

"Interesting. What was the one thing you wanted to tell me, Virgil?"

"As I said, this is the case of a lifetime. Watch for people who should be on your side getting in the way, running interference, or worse, to get a piece of this case and credit and fame that goes with it. That's worth repeating."

Roger said, "Yeah, I'll be on my toes. You make it sound like I have less to fear from Cowboy Gene than I do from some in law enforcement."

"Well said, Roger."

"I'll keep my eyes open for both villains."

They got up. Roger paid the bill, and they walked outside.

"Wish you luck, Roger."

"I'm gonna need it."

They said their goodbyes and got into their vehicles. Virgil Twigg drove off first. Roger followed and saw the former FBI man do a U-turn at the light and head for Titusville. As Roger drove down US 1, he thought of what he'd just been told. He'd had to deal with some backstabbers and glory hogs before, and it hadn't been a fun experience. In the end, he might find he had more empathy for Cowboy Gene than some trying to catch him. You never know. It just might be.

Chapter 19

Roger walked out of his trailer and onto the screened-in porch just in time to see the donkey escaping out the open gate. *How did that get open?* A curse slipped from his lips. "Donkey! You get back here! Where do you think you're going?"

The last time he got loose, he'd found a mare in heat and had a tryst with her. Chief of Police Bill Kenney brought him back after he'd done the dirty deed along with a somewhat drunken owner that made Jed Clampett of the Beverly Hillbillies look high class. Somehow, all had dodged the bullet on that escapade, though a love colt had resulted from the union.

"Donkey, you get back here if you know what's good for you," Roger yelled. He muttered some more curses as he watched the escaped donkey trotting down Canaveral Flats Boulevard. "K9, why did I ever agree to take that dumb ass in? What was I thinking?"

She barked happily. "Yeah, I know. I got more compassion for four-legged critters than I got common sense. Guess I better go get him before he gets in trouble and ends up at a glue factory or put down. You guard the house, okay?"

She yelped again, and Roger exited the porch. He jumped in his truck and took off after the donkey that was still loping down Canaveral Flats Boulevard. He was glad he'd put a halter on him, but how Roger was going to catch donkey and get his cooperation to return was something he'd still have to figure out. Donkey had a good lead on Roger, but he soon caught up. Roger yelled at him, "Stop if you know what's good for you," but the donkey didn't slow down at all.

Donkey took a right on a side street, then a left at the first street, went into a yard, and began to graze. Roger stopped the truck and got out. "Good donkey, good donkey. Don't make this hard on yourself if you know what's good for you," but donkey didn't seem to care. He took a few more bits of grass and took off when Roger got close. Roger followed him to the next yard and then the next, where he walked up to the house and began to eat the flowers. "Donkey, you stop that. You're in enough trouble as it is. Don't make it worse."

The house door opened, and a woman about Roger's age appeared. She had brownish-blonde hair with some gray in it and green eyes that spoke of mischief. She wore a bright yellow colorful sundress and was as flat as a board in front. "What's going on here?" she asked, more curious than angry.

"I'm sorry to bother you, ma'am, but this donkey has escaped his pasture, and I'm trying to get him home."

"So, your donkey has escaped and is now eating my prize-winning flowers?"

"I'm really sorry about that, ma'am. He's not really my donkey. I'm takin' care of him until we can find him a suitable home. I'll pay for the flowers if need be."

She walked down the steps, out the screened porch door, and toward the donkey. "Hey, fellow. Are those good? Please don't eat them all."

Roger could feel the bill for the flowers going up by the second. "Yeah, please, donkey. Don't eat them all," Roger pleaded.

Carefully, she walked up toward the donkey that looked up at her. She stopped for a moment and then continued walking forward. "There, boy," she said as she touched his head. "There, boy. You're a good fellow, aren't you?"

Roger disagreed. *If he were a good fellow, I wouldn't be chasing him over half of Canaveral Flats,* but he kept that to himself.

She stroked the donkey's head. "Good fellow. Why did you cause this fine man so much trouble? Be a good boy and go with him, okay? Back where you belong." She continued to stroke his head and spoke soothing words to him.

Roger handed her a rope that she tied to the donkey's harness. "Good boy."

Roger said, "Can you keep him here while I get my truck? I'll tie the rope to the bumper and walk him back home. Would that be alright?"

"Okay, I'll keep him busy. He seems to want more flowers."

Roger could hear the meter on the flower bill spinning rapidly. It seemed to ding each time it went around. "I'm parked two doors down. I'll make it quick." He worried he might not be able to afford the bill if this went on much longer.

He ran to the dirt street and down to where his truck was parked. Quickly, he returned to the scene of the crime and parked his truck in the driveway of the house next to a red Pontiac Grand Am. Roger took the rope from her and tied it to the back bumper. "Sorry to cause you so much trouble, ma'am. What do I owe you for the flowers he ate?"

She laughed, "You don't owe me anything. I haven't had this much excitement in a long time."

Roger let out a sigh of relief. "Thank you so much. I thought I may have to take out a loan to pay for his damages. My name's Roger Pyles."

"I'm Peggy Sue Tallman. Welcome to my humble abode. I don't get many visitors. My mom's old, and it's all I can do to care for her. Doesn't leave much time for anything else."

"Nice car, you got there."

"My older brother's dealt in cars since he could drive and got it for us. I couldn't afford it if not for his help and what my sister chips in. Mom has a lot of expenses to keep her going."

Roger said, "Yeah, my parents have passed, but I remember how expensive and trying it was in the last years of their lives. Somehow you just got to see it through to the end and do the best you can."

She nodded, "No truer words have ever been spoken, Mr. Pyles."

"Call me, Roger, please."

"Okay, Roger, it is. Call me, Peggy Sue."

"Like in the Buddy Holly song?"

"It is. Now, Roger, I best better be going. Mom should be waking up soon, and I want to have something good prepared and ready for her to eat."

"Okay, thanks for your help and going easy on my wallet and a hungry wayward donkey."

She laughed. "No problem at all. Good luck getting him back home."

"Thank you, Peggy Sue. Maybe we'll meet again."

"Could be. Now I got to be going. Bye." She turned and walked away.

Roger walked to the donkey and said, "You've caused enough trouble for today. Be a good boy, and don't cause any more trouble, okay? And quit bothering good people like the Tallmans. Come along peaceful-like back to my place. You get in too much trouble, and it could be a death sentence for you. Behave yourself."

Donkey gave Roger an "aw shucks" look.

Roger shook his head and mumbled, "Why me, Lord, and why here of all places?" But the sky was silent.

He got in the truck, started it, turned around, and pulled out on the side street. Donkey trotted along behind. Roger found his way back to Canaveral Flats Boulevard and shortly arrived back at his property. He pulled in with donkey still in tow, stopped the truck, got out, and closed the gate. Roger inspected it for damage or some reason why it had been open but found none.

He walked to the donkey and untied him. "Try and behave yourself. And I repeat, I don't want you bothering good law respecting people like the Tallmans. Don't be bothering anyone else, either. They may want you done away with. Do you want that?"

Donkey gave him that "aw shucks" look again.

"Don't you look at me like that. This is serious. If not for nice Peggy Sue, we'd be in a world of hurt."

Donkey put his head down and sauntered off toward his shelter.

Roger shook his head. Yeah, Peggy Sue had done him a big favor. Maybe one day he'd get a chance to return it. You never know what fate has in store.

Chapter 20

Life is never what you expect. Carole's mind was not entirely on her work at the bank as she counted the money out to old Mister Hedrick. No, her thoughts were on the news her son had delivered to his mother and father yesterday. She was too young to be a grandmother. It didn't surprise her that her son had been fooling around with his girlfriend at college. He was a senior, after all, also twenty-two. She remembered that age. Anyone who could count could figure out she'd been pregnant at the altar with the same son. She wasn't happy, but they'd adjust and make it work. Children needed to be born and have a good home. Somehow, they'd make it work out.

A voice brought her back to reality. "You gave me an extra twenty."

"What?"

"You gave me an extra twenty. I think a couple of the new ones stuck together."

Carole sighed, "Thank you for your honesty, Mr. Hedrick. My mind's not totally in the game today."

"Family issues, Carole?"

"Yeah, family issues."

"Those can sure sap your concentration," he said. "Here's the extra twenty back."

"Thank you."

"I'll be praying for you, Carole."

"Thank you, Mr. Hedrick."

Carole liked Mr. Hedrick, an elder at Merritt Island Baptist Church. Even though she and Harold were lapsed Baptists, she still remembered the counseling he'd given them when they were a young struggling couple. Seemed like life's struggles never ended for anyone until life itself ended. He walked away slowly. Mr. Hedrick didn't move as fast as he used to and now needed a cane. An auto accident had left him with a bum knee.

The next person in line stepped in front of her. She knew that face covered with a beard and tinted sunglasses. It was Cowboy Gene. She almost smiled. Life had gotten more interesting. He handed her a note and a bag. Just like the first time, the note said to put lots of money in the bag, no dye packs, no alarms, and no one gets hurt. He knew where she lived.

She placed numerous bundles of dollar bills into the bag and carefully hid the dye pack among them, though he watched her movements like a hungry hawk eyeing a fat mouse. Carole wasn't going to make it easy for him, but he was one step ahead of her. He quickly reached into the back of the bag, pulled out the dye pack, and handed it back to her in his gloved hand. Cowboy Gene even wagged his finger at her before he turned around and exited the bank. She hit the silent alarm as he turned a corner outside of the building and quickly disappeared.

The manager whispered in her ear. He'd noticed she'd hit the silent alarm. She nodded her head. Yes, she'd been robbed. He went to the double doors, locked them, and announced to the remaining customers that they should remain calm. The bank had been robbed. One man looked puzzled. An elderly woman appeared shocked, and a young mother with a toddler in tow pulled her child to her with one arm and placed her hand over her open mouth. The police showed up within a minute, but Cowboy Gene had robbed the bank again and gotten clean away like before.

At home, Carole was very animated as she told her husband, Harold, about being robbed a second time by Cowboy Gene. He listened intently and picked up on her excitement. To celebrate, he took her out to Kelsey's Restaurant in Port St. John. The meal was super, a pepperoni and mushroom calzone and a Greek salad, and they drank far too many mixed drinks for their own good. Harold was glad he didn't see any cops on the way home.

The kids were watching the TV when they got home and barely looked up from their favorite show when their parents floated through the house. After a quick good night to the children, and mom and dad eagerly headed to the bedroom. The door shut quickly with a little slam, but the kids took little notice, and clothing was soon flying everywhere. What a night it would be, one to remember. Why, Carole'd been robbed by Cowboy Gene. Again.

Chapter 21

"Grrrr," K9 growled.

"Yeah, girl, it's our favorite flatfoot on the way here. You know if you bite him, you'll get sick."

She growled again as Bill approached Roger's old trailer.

"Hey, Roger, how's it goin'?" Bill looked at K9, and she growled at him. "And a hello to you, too, K9. Roger treating you okay?" She growled. "I thought so."

"Okay, Bill, what brings you to my humble abode today?"

Bill laughed, "Got time for a stupid criminal story?"

"Sure. What kind?"

"Bank robbery."

"Bank robbery? If it's a stupid bank robbery story, I know it ain't about Cowboy Gene. After fully digesting all the information in his file, I can see why he's gotten away over and over again."

"Nope, not Cowboy Gene. You're right. He's too slick. He may never get caught. He may even steal enough to retire on a beach in Mexico and just disappear. Some have. This story's about a really stupid bank robber, and it's hard to believe."

"Bill, don't keep me in suspense. Sock it to me."

"Sock it to me? You been watching *Laugh-In* on the TV?"

"Yeah, how did you guess?" Roger grinned.

Bill shook his head. "Sock it to me. Roger, you amaze me sometimes."

"My late wife used to say I was amazing."

Bill said sarcastically, "I can't imagine why?"

Roger cleared his throat. "Are you goin' to tell me or keep me in suspense?"

Bill rolled his eyes. "Roger, you truly are amazing. Now, where was I before I was so rudely interrupted? Oh, yeah, dumb bank robber."

Roger said, "I was wondering when you'd get back to that."

Bill ignored the cut. "You know where Oviedo is, don't you?"

"Yeah, out Route 50 going to Orlando."

"Close enough. Well, one of the local guys over there, not the sharpest tack in the box, had a money problem, too little of it, and decided he could solve that problem by robbing a bank. They wouldn't miss a little, you know. He needs a disguise, so he came up with the brilliant idea of an extremely low cost and low-fat disposable disguise. He'd cover his whole head with whipped cream. Why, it was a super idea, went on easy, covered any identifying marks, even his hair color, and came off easy. Also, it tasted good."

Roger said, "An A for innovation, but I have a feeling I'm about to hear a tale of epic failure proportions."

Bill smiled, "Our walking human sundae topping walked into First National of Oviedo. The young woman teller couldn't believe what she was seeing and began to giggle. When he demanded she fill a sack with money, the giggles became open laughter. The whipped cream was getting warm, and it began to slide off his head. She'd long ago hit the silent alarm, and he got wise and walked out. Oviedo is known for the chickens that roam the old downtown area, and when they smelled the whipped cream, they wanted some and attacked our inept bank robber. Before you could say banana split, the Oviedo Police showed up, rescued him from about four chickens pecking away at his head, arrested the dairy delight, and refrigerated him downtown."

"At the cooler?"

"Right again, Sherlock. At the cooler and put him on ice, and he was happy to go with them."

"Naturally," Roger said.

"All units, 10-31 in progress. All available units respond," a disembodied female voice said.

"What's that?" Roger asked.

Bill reached for what was making the noise. "Roger, I'm joining the modern age. This is a police scanner and communicator. The whole county is testing out this new system. So far, it seems to be working well. Take a look at it. It's got a nice strap for easy carrying, too." He handed the device to Roger, who took it.

"I always liked new gadgets. Mind if I look it over closely?"

Bill said, "No, go ahead. You're still a member of the Canaveral Flats Police Force. Have you forgotten?"

"I try to, but you won't let me."

The voice came from the device, "All units, be advised subject is believed to be traveling south on US 1 from Space Coast Credit Union, Port St. John branch."

Bill said, "He's coming my way. I better go help out. Bye."

"What about this thing?" Roger pointed to the police radio.

"Keep it and try to figure it out. I just got it and barely know enough about it to turn it on. Got to answer the call of duty."

"Okay."

Bill ran down to the gate.

"Shut it tight when you're through," Roger yelled.

Bill opened and closed the gate, then gave Roger a thumbs-up, and drove away in his vehicle.

"That Bill would sure make my naughty list if he left the gate open. I don't need the donkey getting out again," Roger said out loud. "I must be goin' crazy. Talkin' to myself and a dog. Oh, well, short drive, and I'll have lots of company."

Roger sat down and read the operating instructions on the radio's case. "Hmm, sounds simple enough. No wonder Bill couldn't figure it out." Roger laughed to himself. He heard K9 whining. "What's up, girl?" A quick look at her food bowl told him the reason. "Empty, how'd that happen?" He opened the metal trash can where he kept her bags of food, and to his surprise, it was empty, too. "K9, we have a problem." She whined pitifully. "I know. I know. I messed up, and you have to suffer. You know K9, I'm almost out of beer, and I need some groceries anyway. I think I need to head for the store." K9 continued to whine. "Okay, I get the picture. Looks like I better do it right now. You guard the house for me, though there's not much here worth stealing, okay? About the only thing worth taking is Bill's radio thingie, and I think I'll take it with me." She yelped and wagged her tail. "K9, there are times I think you actually understand English. I'll be back in a jiffy. Watch the house." She barked again with enthusiasm.

Roger got in his truck, drove to the gate, and opened and closed it when he was through. He didn't need any more donkey chasing fiascoes and proceeded east on Canaveral Flats Boulevard. He hadn't gone far when the radio cracked, "All units, vehicle fleeing bank robbery in Port St. John is believed have turned onto Canaveral Flats Boulevard. Subject vehicle is possibly red in color."

Roger's attention perked up as he continued east on Canaveral Flats Boulevard. Two vehicles passed him, an old pickup truck and a VW Beetle. He saw a car approaching, and it was red. As it passed him, he noted the driver – a man with a beard wearing a cowboy hat and dressed like one. He watched it turn onto a side street. When it did, he made a quick U-turn and followed it down the side street. He could not see it, but he followed the dust trail the vehicle created. The car looked familiar. Where had he seen it before?

He took a right. The neighborhood looked familiar, too. It was where he'd caught up with the escaped donkey. He knew where to go. He pulled down the driveway to where Peggy Sue Tallman lived and looked around carefully. What should he do? He got out of his truck and went to the red car, and felt the hood. It was hot to the touch. Now, what should he do? He thought maybe he would try to call for help on the new radio, but he heard the house door open, and there stood Peggy Sue Tallman in a sundress eyeing him.

"Do you remember me?" he said.

"I do."

Roger tried to sound official. "Good, I'm Roger Pyles, and I'm a member of the Canaveral Flats Police Department. I have reasonable cause to believe a bank robber known as Cowboy Gene is in your house. I'd like to have your permission to search it, but I don't need it."

"He ain't here," she said. "Just me and my mom."

"For your own protection, I need to check that out."

She shrugged, "Whatever," and let him pass into the house.

The small bathroom was in front of him with the door open, and he could see in. It was empty. Roger took a right to the living room. Mrs. Tallman was asleep in a chair. He did a quick sweep of the room, but there was no one else there. A small bedroom, the mother's, also was empty. Carefully, he swung the other bedroom door open and looked around. The bed was immaculately made, and nothing seemed unusual. And empty. He saw no man.

Roger turned to Peggy Sue, who was behind him. "Where is he, Peggy Sue? I know there's a man hiding in here."

"I assure you that the only man here, is you, Roger Pyles. You're wasting your and my time by looking for one."

Roger was beginning to wonder the same. He noted some oversized sunglasses on the dresser top along with two glass dolphins. A closed door of the closet beckoned him. He decided to open it. A man's vest, shirt, and pants were hanging from a hanger along with some women's clothing also on hangers. Roger wondered where the man was hiding, and then he looked up to the dark top shelf. "What the hell?"

He saw a Styrofoam mannequin's head with a beard pinned to it and a cowboy hat on top. With suspicion, he looked at her. Under the bed, he found a bag of money. "Where is he, Peggy Sue? Where's Cowboy Gene? I know he's here."

"I told you. There's no man here. I wouldn't lie about that."

Roger studied her closely and noticed spots of theatre dye in her hair and a faint splotch of glue residue around her mouth. "Well, I'll be damned. You're Cowboy Gene, aren't you?"

She nodded. "I feared this day. I knew that someday despite all my careful planning, something would go wrong." She sighed. "I robbed the bank in Port St. John." She pulled a pack of cigarettes, Virginia Slims, from a pocket in the sundress. "I think I need a smoke." She lit it, inhaled deeply, held it, and then exhaled. "There. Better."

"Why did you do it? Why Peggy Sue? Why?" Roger asked, but she looked away and seemed to be staring at something distant.

"They're coming," she said.

"Who's coming?"

"Having super-sensitive hearing can be a blessing and a curse. Hear them now?"

The low wail of a siren, then two, then a multitude came from the east and rapidly grew closer and closer. Six police cars, mainly from the Brevard County Sheriff's Department, sped into the Tallman house yard. Deputies, mostly men, jumped out of their vehicles with their guns drawn. Roger said, "I'm Roger Pyles of the Canaveral Flats Police Department. Everything's under control. I've captured Cowboy Gene, and he's right here."

The deputies looked puzzled and worked quickly to secure the area. Roger saw Canaveral Flats Chief of Police Bill Kenney among them. He came to the table where the man and woman sat. Roger said, "How did you know to come?"

Bill shook his head. "You big dummy. I knew I should have never left you with that radio. You had the thing in broadcast mode, and everything that you said was heard by every cop in the county. What the hell were you thinking going after a bank robber unarmed alone?"

Roger grimaced. "Guess I wasn't thinking, but I did catch Cowboy Gene, something you guys couldn't do for years."

Now, it was Bill's turn to grimace. "He turned to Peggy Sue Tallman, "You're under arrest for the robbery of Space Coast Credit Union. Anything you say can and will be used against you. Do you understand?"

"I do." She stood up and turned around with her hands behind her back. "You can cuff me now. I won't give you any trouble. Please call my sister and tell her what's happened. Mom needs someone to look after her. Please?"

Bill placed the handcuffs on her, took her to a police car, and put her in the back. He walked back to Roger. Bill said, "I don't know whether to congratulate you for capturing Cowboy Gene or kick your ass into the next county. You could have gotten yourself killed. What if it had been a guy with a gun and an attitude? Where would you be then?"

A chagrined Roger said, "Guess it could have gone south, but I did get our man or woman as it turned out."

"You did catch Cowboy Gene; I give you that, but I'm also gonna make sure you get some training. This line of work can be dangerous."

"Bill, you're preaching to the choir. I'm all in on the training. Now, what happens next here?"

"They send a team out to gather evidence, and they take your statement. You're in for several hours of paperwork."

"I thought so. And Bill."

"What?"

"Please don't try to kick my ass into the next county. Donkey wouldn't like that, and he's likely to put up a big fuss, one you might not like."

Bill picked up on Roger's double meaning. "Gotcha. Never mind. Something I said in the heat of battle. Sorry."

"I thought so. Just wanted to make sure. I could use a beer."

"I could, too, but don't even think about it."

"It was in jest, Bill."

"Jest or not, I think we could both use one."

A deputy came to Roger. "Mr. Pyles, I need to get a statement from you."

"Okay."

Bill said, "I'm not needed here. Better get back to normal cop business, and Roger, give me that radio before it gets you in any more trouble."

"Sure." He handed it to Bill, who walked to his truck and drove off.

Okay, Mr. Pyles. Let's begin…"

An hour later, they were done, and Roger was released. He got in his vehicle and left. *That sure was a surprise. I better get the dog food at Miller's General Store and head home. K9 will be hungry, and I still have a couple of beers in the refrigerator. Wonder what else lies ahead? Guess tomorrow will take care of itself, and I have enough worries for today to deal with. Tomorrow, when it comes, will have its own worries.*

Chapter 22

Two months later

Roger knocked on the door. "Bill, are you here? Bill? Roger rapped again and was about to leave when he saw Bill come staggering out of the bedroom. His eyes were half-open, and his hair was in his face. He stumbled to the door and opened it.

"What do you want? My first day off in weeks. I was trying to catch up on my rest, and you show up like a bad penny. What do you want?"

"It's been a while since I talked to you. Sorry to wake you up. Can I make it up to you? Buy you a meal, and we talk?"

"What time is it, Roger?"

"About 9:30. Where would you like to go?"

"Who said I wanted to go anywhere, you big galoot?" Bill growled, "But seeing how it's on your dime, Mr. Cheapskate, how could I refuse?"

Roger was a little taken back, but he asked, "Where would you like to go? Breakfast place?"

Bill scowled at Roger. "Naw, too late for that. Lone Cabbage opens up at 10:00. I can get something,… and a beer. I sure could use a beer."

"You look like you had a few too many last night."

Bill's eyes shot daggers at Roger. "No," he grumbled. "I'm just tired, and then some yahoo comes pounding on my door, disturbing my beauty rest."

Roger couldn't let that opportunity slip. "Bill, you'd need to sleep like Rip Van Winkle to improve your looks. At least you put on some clothes before you came to the door. Seeing you naked again would probably blind me right off, and if it didn't, I might be tempted to put my own eyes out. There are things I wish I could unsee."

Bill glared, "Remind me again why I like you and shouldn't shoot you."

"Because we've been friends since we were kids, and you don't want to waste a bullet."

"Good points. Give me five minutes to freshen up, and I'll be ready to go. Fair enough?"

"Sounds fine, Bill. I can make some coffee while you get ready. You look like you could use some."

"That's the best news I've heard yet today. Do it while I get ready."

"Okay."

Bill stumbled off to his bedroom, and Roger went into the kitchen and soon had Mr. Coffee perking the elixir of life. Several minutes later, Bill appeared looking much better. "I'm ready."

Roger handed him a large cup of coffee.

"Thanks. I need that bad."

"Got one for me, too," Roger said.

"I figured you would. Let's go."

They walked out of the house, hopped in Roger's vehicle, and headed for the restaurant.

Bill said, "I'm glad the county has been grading the roads regularly. I don't think my head could take five miles of washboard road right now."

"Nor the shocks on this truck. Sorry about getting' you up. I'd thought about comin' over about 7:30. I knew you were usually an early riser, but something told me to wait till I did. How's my cousin Suzy?"

"I haven't hardly seen her lately. We've both been so busy. Guess she's doin' alright."

"Wanna hear a cousin Suzy story?"

"Sure, Roger, I could use something amusing."

"As you know, she lived at my home a while when she was young. My mom kept chickens, and one day a

148

neighbor's peacock came to visit the chickens. Suzy saw it and got my mom. She asked her how she made a chicken bloom like that. I hadn't thought of that story in years."

Bill laughed. That's funny. I could use some more funny today. Like I said, I've been swamped and didn't get in till late. Been working on a serious problem."

"What's that?"

"Corruption in the county involving elections. I'll give you an overview, seeing how you are a member of the Canaveral Flats Police Force, and it involves our little town."

"I'm all ears, Bill."

"About the only place suitable for voting in our little burg is Miller's General Store. Mrs. Miller lets the town do it there for free, and she does like the extra business it brings in on election day. Lester Johnson and Fred, Mrs. Miller's son, oversee the voting."

"So far, so good. Lester is as honest as the day's long, and savant Fred will remember everything that goes on. Where's the problem?"

"I'm getting to that. After all the votes are collected, the ballot box is sealed. I personally took the ballots to the central office in West Cocoa to be tabulated. They signed to accept the box. I still have the receipt. A month ago, someone drove a stolen car into the pond by the building. When it was brought out, a box that contained ballots was dragged out, too. And after draining the swamp, many boxes of ballots were found, including all those from Canaveral Flats. None of the boxes had ever been opened and counted. The discarded ballots all seemed to come from areas in the county that vote pretty much one way, and that's not the way those in power would like. Roger, this county has had big problems in the past with matters like this, and I believe this could be just the tip of the iceberg. The governor's already removed the Brevard Supervisor of Elections and doing what he can to get rid of anything that has the appearance of impropriety, but it's an uphill battle. I fear with the various systems of counting votes in the sixty-seven counties of this state, questions about who won the elections will come up again."

"That is serious. Old tyrant Joseph Stalin is reported to have said something like this, 'Never mind how the people vote. What's important is who counts the votes.'"

"There were other problems, too, Roger. The building next door had been burglarized in the past, and they put up cameras outside recently. One of them had a partial view of the election's office loading bay. The video we got showed a white unmarked box van pull up about 4 A.M. and dropped off trash cans and garbage bags full of what we believe were ballots. One bag ripped open, and people were seen, nervously and hurriedly, gathering them up. Roger, things look rotten in Brevard. I don't know if we'll ever get to the bottom of this and if anyone will go to jail. It's hard to prove when months have gone by, elections have been certified, and time moves on. I only fear it will get worse in the future with more electronic ballots and no paper trail.

"The last election at one voting place in Miami, 3000 votes were found already entered into a machine when they opened up the place. The poll watchers refused to certify the results, and somehow the officials there got away with sweeping it under the rug. I know this has happened in more places than just Miami."

Roger said, "Sounds serious."

"Yeah, they managed to dry out some of the ballots. The results would have swung several elections, and God only knows about the ballots brought in in the dead of night. There's something rotten in Denmark and Brevard County and other places. I've been so busy with this and my usual duties. I know how a one-armed paperhanger feels."

"What's the news on Peggy Sue Tallman, a.k.a. Cowboy Gene, Bill?"

"The state let her plead guilty to the one charge of robbing the Space Coast Credit Union. She threw herself on the mercy of the court. Her attorney claimed crazy middle-aged woman's hormonal problems. He said it wouldn't happen again. She didn't have so much as a parking ticket against her. The judge bought it, and she got two years in prison with credit for time served in the county jail. Actually, I think there was a lot of pressure from the state to try and put this all behind us. After she ran circles around them, they'd like this whole matter dropped and forgotten. With good behavior, she could be a free woman in a year, year and a half tops."

Roger said, "Aw, the wheel of justice. Hard to figure out sometimes. Still she seemed like a harmless, nice lady with a good heart."

"Agreed. No one in that family ever gave me any problems in all the years they lived in Canaveral Flats. It's hard to figure out."

"It is. Oh, one more thing. Got a letter from the governor thanking me for my help with Cowboy Gene. He said he may need my services again sometime if I was available."

Bill said, "That's good to know."

"And I found the check he had promised, and there was even a bonus in it."

"Roger, that's surprising. I think he's happy to see an end to the Cowboy Gene bank-robbing debacle. Everyone in law enforcement would like to forget this confused fiasco."

"Well, here we are, no more dirt road." Roger took a right on Florida Route 520, and soon they were at Lone Cabbage Fish Camp and Restaurant. He pulled into a parking spot near the highway, and they got out.

Bill said, "You go ahead. I see Pastor Nassey getting in his car. I need to speak to him. You go on. Tell the waitress I want my usual. This should take but a minute or two."

"Okay."

Roger walked into the old building and found a seat by the window, looking over the St. Johns River. It looked a little lower than what he'd remembered. He grabbed a menu and found something that appealed to him. At about that time, a waitress showed up.

"Well, hello. Good to see you again. How are you, Roger?"

"Sugar Plum? Is that you?"

"Yup. FYI, I'm doin' fine. You ready to order?"

"Yeah, I want a number 2 with fries and two beers, Yuenglings. I'm with Bill Kenney. He should be here in a jiffy and told me to tell the waitress, that being you, to get him his usual, okay?"

"Okay, two number 2's with fries. Two West Virginia style hot dogs coming up. Anything else, Roger?" She winked at him.

"No, I think I'm good for now. Not speaking for wild Bill."

She smiled, "Gotcha, I'll put your order in and get your beers."

She left and disappeared into the kitchen. Roger watched several people in boats fishing on the nearby river for some time. Didn't seem like the fish were biting. Bill showed up and sat down. He said, "Got the order in?"

"Yeah, hot dog with coleslaw and chili. Fries, too, and a beer."

153

"That'll work, Roger. What did you get?"

"The same."

"Good choice."

Roger asked, "What was the pastor doin' here?"

"Went fishing, but they weren't biting. The restaurant got his fish for him today, already breaded and cooked just right.."

"Bill, what did you need to talk to him about today?"

"Part of the investigation about the ballots in the pond. The county uses the church for a polling place, and the pastor told me he personally sealed the ballot box, took it to the Office of Elections, and has the receipt they gave him when he dropped them off. Those ballots cast at the church were also in the pond. The people in this area aren't happy with the powers that be and generally vote the other way."

"More evidence of voter fraud."

Bill nodded, "So it appears. I wish that surveillance tape we had also covered the side door, but it doesn't. That would make it real easy to see who did the dumping."

"Sure would. If wishes were horses, beggars would ride."

Bill laughed, "Yeah, I don't know if anyone will go to jail. Few ever do. They plan and cover their tracks well.

Still, some heads are goin' to roll. The governor has ordered the head person in charge of the count gone also, and it remains to be seen how many the sweep will catch."

"So, you think this is the work of the party in power? Seems like that bunch is okay with corruption and will do whatever it takes to keep power," Roger said.

"True, but the lust for power and greed can be equal opportunity seekers. Years ago, before you moved here, a sheriff a few counties down, not a member of the party in question here, campaigned with the slogan, 'I control all crime' in the said county. He did alright. If he wasn't getting a piece of the action one way or the other, it didn't happen. Got so bad, the governor had him removed and arrested. He went to jail for a while, and last I heard moved to a small town in Colorado and did the same thing there. I think he stole a large amount of money from the town treasury and headed for the border. Think they're still looking for him."

"Oh, what a tangled web we weave when first we practice to deceive."

Bill said, "Shakespeare isn't it?"

"It's commonly credited to him, but it was actually from a poem called Mariom, A Tale of Flodden Field by Sir Walter Scott. You may need that info if you ever get on Jeopardy."

Bill laughed, "Fat chance of that."

"What you gonna do with the rest of your day?"

"Well, I'm up now. Suzy asked me to secure a shelf that was working loose. Guess I'll do that and try to get a nap this afternoon if I'm not disturbed."

Roger said, "You still not messin' with her, are you?"

Bill gave Roger a dirty look. "I told you I don't mix business and pleasure, almost never, but no, I'm not." He paused. "How's it goin' with Hernandez and your kid?"

"About the same, but we made a little progress. Hoping for more little by little. Suzy's still helping with his therapy. Say, where's our stuff? It should have been here by now."

Another waitress arrived with their beers. "Sorry for the long wait, guys. Sugar Plum left in a hurry. Some kind of family issue she's been dealing with. Your food should be up very soon."

Bill said, "Sorry to hear that. Thanks for the update."

Roger said, "Yeah, I hope it works out. Family issues can really take a toll on a person."

"It sure can," she said. They heard a bell ding. "Looks like your foods ready. I'll be right back with it." She returned quickly and sat the dogs and fries in front of them. "Enjoy."

"We will," Bill said.

Roger nodded, and she left. He said, "Family issues. Something I wouldn't wish on anyone, but seems like everyone has to deal with them."

"Ain't that the truth. Let's eat." And so they did, and it was good.

Roger asked, "Any last thoughts, Bill?"

A mischievous smile came to Bill's face. "Yeah, Titan Uranus."

"What? Have you gone kinky on me? Tighten your anus?"

"No, Titan Uranus."

"You better explain yourself, Bill. Not sure I want to be in the same truck with you. Got another way home?"

Bill shook his head. "I'm messing with you. Let me explain. I was over at Port Canaveral, having lunch at Fischer's Restaurant, and I looked across the channel to where the ships are. An oil tanker was being unloaded, and its name was 'Titan Uranus.' That's spelled T-i-t-a-n U-r-a-n-u-s. I pointed that out to the waitress. She told me the ship comes in with a load of oil about once a month. It's owned by some Asian company where English isn't the first language. Everyone at the port has a laugh when it comes in. You might call it the butt of jokes."

"Titan Uranus. Not a ship I'd care to ride on."

"Nor me, Roger. Sorry about the joke, but I couldn't help myself."

Roger laughed, "I'd have had some fun with you, too, Bill, if I'd seen it first. Let's get out of here. I know we both have things we need to do."

"That's a fact."

"And by the way, Bill."

"What?"

"Titan Uranus."

Bill laughed. "Let's go."

They went to the cash register, and Roger paid the bill. He took Bill back to his house. As he rode back to his trailer, he pondered on developments. *It's a rotten old world we live in. And it ain't over until the fat lady sings. Wonder if she's even warming up?* He laughed to himself. *Titan Uranus.* Sometimes well-meaning ideas and plans can get you in a world of unintended trouble.

Chapter 23

Ten months later.

Why is it that I always pick the cart with the bad wheel? Doesn't this place have any decent carts? Roger groaned. *Why me, Lord? Why me? What else can go wrong? I had a flat tire on the way here and had to fix it in a downpour. And the spare barely had any air. Glad Hogan's Union gas station was close, and the air pump actually worked. Why me, Lord?*

His cart was about half-full now. It pushed hard and pulled to the right. He rounded the end of an aisle and crashed hard into another cart. Roger mumbled a curse. "Sorry, ma'am. Are you okay?"

"I think so. No harm done. How about you?"

"I'm okay. Stupid cart's got bad wheels. It rolls hard and pulls to one side."

She said, "Took me three tries to find a good one." Her eyes narrowed. "Say, aren't you Roger Pyles?"

"I am." He looked at her closely. "You look familiar. Do I know you?"

159

"Yeah, I went to prison because of you."

Roger grimaced, and she smiled. "Actually, I went to prison for bank robbery. You were the one who caught me. Don't you remember me? I'm Peggy Sue Tallman."

"What? I thought you were still in the women's prison up Ocala way. What happened?"

She smiled, "First off, Mr. Pyles, no hard feelings. You were just doing your job. I don't hold grudges like some people. Secondly, why am I here and not still in prison? My sister was caring for our mom, who has Alzheimer's, while I was away. Sis got sick and couldn't take care of mom anymore. My lawyer got a judge to agree to my release, so I could provide for her.

"I'd have gotten out sooner, but some idiot found a bomb left over from WW II in an old bombing range in the Ocala National Forest and brought it to his home next door to the prison. Took 'em nearly a week to figure out what to do with it and not get anyone killed.

"I told them they didn't need to be concerned about catching Cowboy Gene again. Me and him will never go back to prison. They got me on a short leash. I can only go to the grocery store, church, and my parole office. The latter is only once a month, so it's not so bad. Far better than prison."

"I hadn't heard you were out. I'm surprised."

She said, "That makes two of us. Life has a way of taking unexpected turns."

"Ain't that the truth? Call me, Roger. Mr. Pyles is too formal."

"Okay, Roger, it is."

"Could you guys have your meet and greet somewhere else, please? You're blocking the way," a stout, short woman asked. She gave them a hairy eyeball.

"Okay," Roger said, and they moved out of the way. "Peggy Sue, I've wanted to talk with you if I ever got the chance. How about we do our shopping and then meet up at the Black Cat Café two doors down?"

She thought for a moment. "It can't be for too long. The neighbor lady watching my mom has to go soon."

"My treat," Roger said.

"That answers my second question. I only have enough for groceries, nothing extra. Money's pretty tight for us now. Coffee and a donut for me."

"Any more questions?"

"A coffee shop isn't on my list of places to be. You know that?"

"If anyone asks, you're on official business with a member of the Canaveral Flats Police Department. That will keep you out of trouble. You can trust me."

"I believe I can."

Roger said, "Any more questions?"

"No questions. Just this – I only answer the questions if I want to."

Roger said, "I thought that might be the case. Deal. Fifteen – twenty minutes work for you?"

"That should do it. See you then, Roger. Got some shopping to do."

"Same here. See you shortly. Bye."

Roger got the rest of what he wanted in the store, including some frozen items. At the checkout, he asked for them to be all in the same bag to help keep things cold. The bagboy grunted and did as he was asked. Roger took his purchase to his truck, set them in the cab on the floor where the passenger's feet would be, and walked to the café. He got two coffees and four donuts. The store had a special on, buy three and get the fourth free. He'd wanted two, and he could take the extra to K9 or eat it later.

He watched Peggy Sue put her supplies in the trunk of an older model car. He noticed a bag of adult diapers. Getting old was no fun. Peggy Sue walked to the coffee shop, came in, and looked around. Roger hollered, "Over here."

She saw him, walked over, and sat down. "Did you think I wouldn't show?"

"No, I believed you would. I got what you asked for."

"Thank you." She took a sip and a bite. She nodded, "Good."

"Yeah, I hope this place makes it. It's an uphill battle for a place like this to stay in business with all the regulations put on them. If the politicians had some skin in the game, maybe it would be different."

Peggy Sue nodded.

"How's your mother doin'?"

"Not very well." She looked down. "My sister isn't doing so well either. Occasionally, I almost wish I was back in prison, but that passes. Even with my problems, it's still better on the outside. Prison's no picnic. Yesterday was mom's birthday. I asked her what she would like. She was in one of her rare lucid times. Mom told me not to get any more knickknacks for the house. Just give her a kiss. She didn't need to dust it." Peggy Sue stopped to whip away a tear. "I wish I had more helping hands, but with mom, sometimes I find the best help I can give her is just by holding her hand in mine." Peggy Sue looked like she was about to break down, but she managed to keep it together.

"You gonna make it, Peggy Sue?"

"I think so." She sniffed and wiped her nose with a napkin. "I try to have a plan to make the most of what I have and then do it."

"You gonna behave yourself and make it through this?"

She smiled, "I think you know me. You know the answer to that question." She took another sip and a big bite of the donut.

"I only have one more question, and your answer will either be long or very short."

"Shoot."

"Why did you do it?"

She smiled weakly and looked away at something distant outside. After a moment, she spoke, "Any more questions?"

"No. I think you've told me enough. Peggy Sue, I wish you the best and hope it all does work out for you."

She smiled, "It will. I know it will."

"For your sake, I hope it does. I really do."

"Thanks, Roger. I think I better be going. Duty calls. Bye." She got up and walked out with her coffee in her hand. Roger watched her drive off. He hoped it all would work out for her, but he had his concerns.

Chapter 24

Two months later

Roger sat on his porch. K9 slept nearby. He had a cat on his lap that wanted attention, and he was trying to read a short book by Louis L'Amour, *Hondo*, when the phone rang. Roger let it go to the answering machine. *Probably some salesman trying to sell me something I don't need.*

"Roger, if you're there, would you please pick up? This is Virgil Twigg. I've got some information on Cowboy Gene you need to know about. It's rather important. Pick up, please."

Roger put down the book and carefully reached for the phone. He didn't want to disturb the cat. "Hello, Virgil. Roger here. Sorry I didn't pick up. I figured it was the usual nuisance sales call. What's up? I thought Cowboy Gene was history."

"Afraid not. The saga continues."

"Fill me in. The last I knew, Peggy Sue Tallman was busy taking care of her invalid mother."

"Her mother died a month ago. Went peacefully in her sleep. When Miss Tallman went to her monthly parole meeting, she was informed she would have to complete the rest of her prison term starting in two weeks' time. She seemed to take it well, but instead, she's disappeared, and someone matching Cowboy Gene's description has been robbing banks all over the state. He's hit banks in St. Augustine, Jacksonville, Tallahassee, and Marianna and got away each time."

"And the police are sure it's Cowboy Gene?"

"Yup, it's almost like she's toying with them, daring them to catch her."

"Could be. There does seem to be a pattern here. Seems like she's heading west."

"The boys in blue think so, too. Every agency west of Marianna to Pensacola is on the alert. Think they'll catch her? Roger, I'd give them a fifty-fifty chance. What do you think?"

"I wouldn't give them that. She's slick and learns from her mistakes. I'm surprised I hadn't heard about it on the radio or seen it in the newspaper."

Virgil said, "They've managed to keep a lid on it so far. Some people would actually root for her success. They see her as a Bonnie without a Clyde, a sort of Robin Hood character."

"I can understand that, but I don't think they can keep it quiet for long."

"Me neither." Roger heard Virgil sigh. "I'd hoped we'd heard the last of Cowboy Gene."

Roger said, "I did, too, but I had my own apprehensions if we'd seen the last of the bandit." He stopped. "So, now what?"

"You may get a call on this, but I doubt it. You solved the case, and now it's unsolved, back to open. The powers that be probably want to keep your name out of this. Understand?"

Roger said, "I believe I do. I'll stay out of the way unless asked to help. Would you keep me in the loop if something breaks, Virgil?"

"I can do that. As they say, it ain't over till it's over."

"That's for sure. That's all I have, Roger. I'll give you a call if I have more."

"Thanks, Virgil. You have a good day. You sure made mine interesting."

"Ain't that the truth? Bye, Roger."

"Take care, Virgil. Bye."

Roger heard a click as the call ended. This was somewhat of a surprise. Peggy Sue and Cowboy Gene were back on the lam. He wondered how this would end. As Virgil had said, it ain't over till it's over. And he pondered what part if any, he'd play in the final act of this chronicle.

Chapter 25

Carole couldn't believe her luck. Why, she'd been robbed by the infamous Cowboy Gene, not once, not twice, but three times, and the bank had even moved her to their branch in downtown Cocoa. Some might say it was bad luck, but she enjoyed the excitement. She was rooting for him, but it was her job to keep him on his toes. The first time she faced him, she'd been so surprised and overwhelmed by what was happening, she'd forgotten to put the dye pack in the money she'd given him. The second time, she'd remembered, but he'd looked, found it, given it back to her, smiled, and shook his index finger at her before turning and casually walking out of the bank.

No, this time was different. Somehow, he looked not quite the same. He seemed a little shorter, not as sure of himself, and she thought he had his cowboy hat on backward, but what did she know about how men wore cowboy hats? She'd slipped the dye pack in the bundles of money because that was her job, and she wasn't going to make it easy on Cowboy Gene. She smiled as she thought about how she'd wanted to make him better as a bank robber; give him a challenge, but he'd failed her test, and that disappointed her.

He took the money, never looked in the bag, and even said thank you before heading for the exit where the security system triggered the dye pack. The money would be useless covered in dye, and it would be easy to identify him. What would she do for excitement now?

His voice had been a surprise. He'd never spoken a word before, and it sounded higher than she expected, almost feminine. The police who came quickly hadn't been interested in talking with her or anyone else there but had taken off in a hurry after getting a call that a concerned citizen who'd witnessed the escape was following the getaway vehicle at a discrete distance. Only one cop was left to secure the bank and keep order until more help to process the scene could arrive. Maybe this time, Cowboy Gene had gotten too confident and had made a mistake or even maybe two. Maybe this time he'd get caught, but she hoped not. Just what would she do for excitement? She sighed.

Maybe she'd get robbed again by another thief sometime in the future, but no one could replace the feeling she'd gotten when Cowboy Gene showed up and changed her life. No, there'd never be another robber like him, and secretly, she hoped he got away and lived long on his ill-gotten gains, but she doubted he would. He may not even survive this day.

Later, she'd be questioned by investigators concerning the robbery, but she kept any mention of the anomalies she'd noticed about Cowboy Gene to herself. Was it really him or a copycat? She didn't want to know.

Murder of Cowboy Gene

She wanted to live thinking she'd been robbed, not once, not twice, but three times by the infamous Cowboy Gene.

Chapter 26

A plume of purple-red smoke rose from the satchel Cowboy Gene carried as he ran from the bank. There was a tremendous amount of money in the bag, ten grand or more. Should he keep it or not? Surely, he could salvage at least half of it. He could ditch it and get away much easier without give-away smoke coming from the bag, but… He decided the risk was worth it.

He hurried to the Holiday Rambler RV he'd parked two blocks from the bank on the quiet side street. After a quick look around, he decided no one was following him, but you never know. Cowboy Gene got in and started the old vehicle up. In his haste for a speedy departure, he nearly collided with a Cocoa Water Department truck. The driver, a black man of middle age, shouted some angry words at him.

From the side street, he pulled on Forrest Street that had one time been US 1 years ago before it was rerouted. He stopped at a red light at State Route 520 and noticed an old station wagon, a woody at that, pull up behind him closely. He looked into his driver's rearview mirror and saw the driver eyeing the RV suspiciously. A car door slammed shut, and in the other mirror, he watched a woman bolt to a payphone nearby. He watched as she dialed and spoke excitedly to someone, all the while looking and pointing at his RV. He didn't like the looks of it.

The light changed, and the old RV lumbered north on Forrest Street and merged onto US 1. The station wagon followed closely. Cowboy Gene had to stop for the light at the Dixon Boulevard intersection. He looked left across the Florida East Coast Railroad tracks and saw a Cocoa Police car sitting idling. *Probably filling out paperwork.* He didn't like it when it sped off through the parking lot in front of Publix and turned right onto Dixon Boulevard coming his way.

The light changed, and he continued his getaway, hoping the cop had a call someplace else. A quick look in the mirror told him to expect trouble. The cop blew through the intersection, nearly causing an accident, and turned north on US 1, and now he had his lights on and was rapidly gaining on the motor home. Cowboy Gene said a few choice words. He could feel the blood rushing in his veins as he considered his options of escape, continue on US 1, turn on Florida Route 528 to Merritt Island, or pull over and surrender.

Option three was out. He was not going back to prison. Option two wasn't so great either. He could get trapped on Merritt Island. Besides, he didn't have the correct change for the tolls. He laughed to himself as that thought brought a little comic relief to his dire situation. It would be US 1, come what may, hope for the best. As he drove under the 528 overpass, two police cars, one a Cocoa city car and one a Brevard County Sheriff's Department vehicle, slid across US 1 and blocked the highway going north.

Too late, he saw what was happening. He could have turned on the westbound exit to 528, but not now. He was running out of options. It was stop, ram a car, or try to make the Highpoint Drive. He chose the latter and nearly rolled the RV with the dangerous right turn. The old vehicle lumbered up the steep street in the upscale neighborhood. A look in the mirrors told him the two cop cars that had blocked his path were now following him in hot pursuit if you could call it that. Black smoke poured from the RV tailpipe as it crested the spot known as Highpoint, eighty-eight feet above sea level, the highest elevation in the county, and the whole Florida East Coast, the remnant of an ancient sand dune when this was the Atlantic Ocean's shore.

He slammed his foot on the brake and slid to a halt. There ahead at the street's intersection with Westchester Drive sat a Cocoa Police car, lights flashing, blocking his path. *Now, what to do?* The cops had their guns out, pointing them at the vehicle. He saw several residents come out their front doors to see what all the commotion was about, but the cops yelled at them to go back inside, which they did, though he could see them peeking out their window through the curtains, one holding a video camera. He shut the engine off and set the parking brake, then pulled the curtains closed. He needed time to think.

Chapter 27

More cops had arrived. Some had rifles. Others had standard pistols, but all were pointed at the RV. After pulling the curtains closed, Cowboy Gene lit a cigarette and sat at the kitchen table. The situation had gone from bad to worse, and he knew there was no way out. Well, there was one way. Cowboy Gene's head nodded, and then he exhaled deeply. "Yup, one way out."

The head nodded again. The die had been cast. The Rubicon would be crossed. There was no turning back. He took a long drag on the cigarette, held it in, and let it out slowly. "No turning back."

From outside, a voice shouted over a bullhorn, "Make it easy on yourself. Give up. Come on out. We've got you surrounded. There's no escape this time, Cowboy Gene."

Cowboy Gene looked around. The satchel sat at his feet. A quick look inside told him the money was useless. It was all stained from the dye. He took another puff from the cigarette, held it in; it felt so good, and then let the smoke drift out his nostrils. He crushed it out in the ashtray.

He walked to the bedroom and opened a drawer. Inside was a .357 Magnum loaded with hollow-point bullets, an efficient killer, but he didn't touch the gun. Instead, he picked up a realistic-looking toy pistol and laid it on the top of the dresser. Then he disrobed. He sat the hat on the Styrofoam head, pulled off the fake beard, laid it in the drawer over the pistol, and took off the sunglasses. He removed the oversized cowboy boots and sat them in the closet. Next went the shirt, vest, and blue jeans. They were folded neatly and laid on the bed. He began to unroll the elastic bandage that held the towel in place, making it look like he had a slight potbelly. Those items went next to the other clothes on the bed.

Cowboy Gene looked in the mirror at the person wearing the pink panties. "Girl, you sure made a mess of things this time. Go out like you really are." She looked at the scars on her chest from the double mastectomy and frowned. "Life's not fair."

From the drawer, she pulled a bra made especially for women who had lost their breasts to cancer, one with C cups. She frowned. *No, the D cup one was the right one today.* She wanted to go out with a bang and not be mistaken for anything other than a woman.

She put it on and adjusted the straps until they were comfortable, and she looked right, not lopsided. Her hand reached back into a dresser drawer, and out came a bright yellow sundress she put over her head and pulled down. Comfortable loafers on her feet and a wide rim hat finished her outfit. A quick look in the mirror brought a smile to her face. "Why, you look almost like the old you, happy without a care in the world. What happened? How did it ever get to this?"

She frowned. She knew the answer.

She walked to the kitchen, lite another cigarette, found a notepad and pencil, sat down, and began to write –

"To whom it may concern.

"The last will and testimony.

"Let it be known I committed all the bank robberies that have been attributed to me and a few more. Let's hope my death puts an end to this. I've been to prison for my deeds already, and I'm not going back for a long sentence. I'd prefer it this way. If I was lucky, I might be able to see the sky from the prison yard a few hours a day. That's not living. I want to feel the sun on my face, especially to enjoy its setting into the sea daily. I might even be released before I die in that horrible place, and I don't want to end up like that."

She heard a male voice call over a bullhorn, "Come out with your hands up. We don't want to have to come in there and get you. Do everyone a favor and surrender peacefully."

She frowned. *I wish it were that easy, but you just don't know…*

She continued writing –

"To the police here today. I alone am responsible for my actions, no one else. It was my choice to force you to do what you had to do, your duty. Please don't blame yourselves for making you do what you must. Again, I alone am responsible for my death, no one else. It would break my heart to know you blamed yourself for my choice. I want no one to carry the guilt for my decision.

"I know there is no way out but one. As I sit here, I think of better days behind and better days ahead. I remembered the teachings I heard in Sunday School when I was young – Jesus loves me this I know. I made my peace with Him just now, and I don't fear tomorrow though I fear what will happen shortly. I pray it's quick.

"Everything in this world, I leave to my brother. A word of caution, the gun in the clothes dresser in the bedroom is loaded and has a light trigger. I don't want anyone hurt."

She took a long drag on the cigarette, held it one last time, and let it out. It was almost time.

"Tell my family I love them all, even that brother I had a falling out with. It was over nothing important I now see. I wish I'd had the good sense to say that before now. Better late than never. I guess we all have our regrets."

"Come out, Cowboy Gene. We don't want anyone to get hurt," the voice on the bull horn said.

She signed the letter, looked at what she had written, erased the second name, and signed again in that spot. "There, that's better." She put out the cigarette, walked to the door, and opened it. "You're going to have to kill me."

The cops couldn't believe what they were seeing. A woman old enough to be their mother was standing there with her hands on her hips. "Who the hell is that?" one startled cop said to another crouched next to him.

"Must be Cowboy Gene's girlfriend," he replied.

"You don't have to do this, Ma'am. Give yourself up," yelled the man.

"So, if I come out with a gun in my hand and point it at you guys, you aren't going to shoot me?"

"Please, please don't do that," he begged.

She disappeared into the RV and got the realistic toy gun. She prayed, "Father, thank you for forgiving me for all I've done and about to do. I'll see you soon. Please don't hold it against them for what I made them do. Comfort them. They'll need it more than I do and will. Amen."

She was at peace when she walked out of the RV door with the pistol in her hand. Multiple shots rang out almost immediately, and she crumbled to the pavement face first. Most hit her in the chest, but one struck her face. Somehow she found the strength to roll to her side, lift her head, and look at the sun though blood ran into her eyes. Quiet returned to the neighborhood, and a squirrel chirped his disapproval of the racket. She looked at the unhappy rodent, and a Cocoa cop thought he saw a slight smile on her pained face. And then, she closed her eyes and departed this life.

Chapter 28

Marie couldn't believe what she was reading in *Florida Today*. Her friend from high school was dead. Peggy Sue had gone back to her old ways, and fate had finally caught up with her. She remembered when she had limped back into Cocoa after her adventure to California years ago. She'd run into her at a local fast food restaurant where Peggy Sue had found a job. They talked when she'd gotten a break. It bothered Marie that she'd taken up smoking, but Peggy Sue blew it off literally. Bad for your health and hard on your pocket. Peggy Sue just smiled and laughed it off. She still had that smile, but something was different about her, though Marie couldn't put her finger on it. Something was different; Marie was sure.

It was almost like old times when they got together for a night on the town. With her long legs and winning smile, Peggy Sue never had to worry about getting attention from the opposite sex. There was always some guy willing to buy them drinks as a pretense to get to know them and maybe more, but Peggy Sue never seemed to trust men. Oh, she knew they had sex on their minds, but it was something more elementary that caused Peggy Sue to keep her distance from the suitors.

Peggy Sue had done some crazy things when they went drinking during nights on the town. She'd found a '57 Chevy convertible all decked out with the keys still in the ignition. What a time that was driving from Merritt Island across the Route 528 Indian River Bridge, down US I through Cocoa, then back across the river on the south bridge back to Merritt Island, over to Cocoa Beach, up A1A, and finally to the bar on Courtenay Boulevard. She could still feel the wind blowing through her hair, especially the salty air along the beach. What a night that was.

When they pulled into the bar lot, the car's owner came running with a cop following closely. After the initially heated outburst, Peggy Sue managed to sweet-talk him out of pressing charges. Why, they'd filled up the tank and returned it undamaged, as good as new. He told the cop not to bother with charging her for her little joy ride. No foul, no harm done. She even dated him a few times, enjoying him treating her and riding around in his convertible on his dime. He thought she owed him and was going to make a big score, hit a home run, but she never let him get to first base. Marie knew because they laughed about it. Peggy Sue thought it funny how it worked out. Somehow, she always seemed to skate on issues like that, get off smelling like a rose. Other than the short stint in prison, she had, till now. Marie felt her head spin a little. It just couldn't be.

She remembered when they worked together for a short time at the marina and how she'd cared for the crippled duck that showed up one day. Peggy Sue said he looked like a Bruce, and so he became. He never had to worry about starving when Peggy Sue was his provider, but his benefactor couldn't protect him from the world. One day, he just wasn't there. They looked the area over but only found a single feather, and they weren't sure it was from him. Maybe a hungry shark or gator got him when he went for a swim. Maybe an osprey or eagle did him in. Maybe a hungry dog. He'd simply disappeared with no forwarding address.

Marie remembered how she heard a noise in the ladies' room at the marina and discovered Peggy Sue crying. Marie made a quiet, hasty retreat. When Peggy Sue came out of the restroom, her eyes were red, but she had her composure back. That was Peggy Sue. She had a good heart, always looking out for the underdog and downtrodden. Marie remembered seeing her give money to a homeless man who had mental issues and had been in prison. She cared about everyone, especially the ones society tried not to see. That was the Peggy Sue Marie knew. She wouldn't hurt a fly.

***

Now here she was at the cemetery. Marie laid a bundle of white roses on the heaped-up fresh dug earth that covered Peggy Sue's coffin along with a bottle of beer in memory of the good times. It was a sad but also good graveside service. Why did she choose to go out that way? She thought she knew. Her family and friends shared stories of Peggy Sue that made everyone smile and laugh. Her brother'd read some scriptures that told of the resurrection of the dead and a better life in heaven when our mortal days are done.

And then she crumbled to her knees, and tears flowed like rain from a Florida summer thunderstorm. She cried until her emotions were spent. Marie sat down and took the cold beer in her hand. She twisted the top off and took a big drink, then poured some on the grave. "Here's to you, Peggy Sue. To the good times."

She drank some more, poured a little on the ground covering her friend, and finished off the bottle. "To the good times, Peggy Sue. It sure was a hell of a ride. Till we meet again. I loved you like the sister I never had."

Chapter 29

Summer 1988

A white car stopped in front of Roger's trailer. It found a wide spot and parked in the grass along Canaveral Flats Boulevard, and a man of about 45 got out. He had a crew cut and wore blue jeans and a T-shirt with Brevard Community College Titans printed on it. He yelled, "Mr. Pyles, is that you? I'm Pete Tallman. I called you and set up this meeting."

"You found the right place," Roger yelled back. "Come on down."

"Does your dog bite?"

"Only people she don't like, and she doesn't know you, so I think you're safe."

"How about the donkey?"

"Maybe I better come up there and let you in. Donkey can be a bit protective."

Roger stroked the back of the tortie cat lying on his lap. "Patches, I'm gonna have to get up. I've got company, and Donkey's in guard mode. Be a good kitty and cooperate. He gently picked her up and sat her on the floor. "Good kitty. Good girl."

Roger crawled out of the La-Z-Boy chair and went out the door, followed by his dog K9 and the cat. The latter dug a small hole, squatted down in it, did her business, quickly covered it up, and ran under the trailer.

Donkey trotted over, and Roger stroked his head. "Now, Donkey, I have a guest. No biting or trampling allowed, you hear? He's not some secret agent or renegade out to do me harm."

Roger opened the gate. "Come on in. We'll talk down at the trailer. You told me just enough on the phone to pique my interest. I'm anxious to hear more."

Pete said, "I was more worried about the dog, but you make it sound like the donkey's the real threat. Were you serious?"

"I was. Donkey's very protective. He showed up in Canaveral Flats some time ago. We never have figured out if he was lost or abandoned, and our local lawman found him. The county animal people had no place for him and wanted to put him down, so I agreed to keep him until we could find him a home. He's been here ever since, thinks this is his home, and it's his job to protect everyone here though he and the dog just tolerate each other. I got K9 at the pound."

Pete said, "Seems like there's a story behind each story."

"Yup, it makes life interesting."

They walked to the screened-in room attached to the trailer and went in. "Take a chair. Would you like something to drink? I got water, Cokes, tea, and beer. What would you like?"

"Some cold water would be fine."

"Okay." Roger pointed to a plastic chair. "Take a seat, and I'll be right back with liquid refreshments." He went into the trailer and soon returned with a bottle of water for Pete and a bottle of Yuenglings beer for himself. "Here you go." He handed the bottle to the other man.

"Thank you." He looked at the bottle. "Knobley Mountain Spring Water. Never heard of them."

"I got it from a friend of mine from up north," Roger said. "Now, what was it you needed to talk with me about today?"

"Some things have been bothering me since the death of my sister, and I thought it best I get with you and tell you about them."

"Okay, shoot. I'm all ears."

"When all this hit the fan, I'm not sure I was thinking clearly. When I heard Peggy Sue had gotten killed after robbing a bank, I think I was in shock. I couldn't believe she'd gone back to that. It was even harder to believe than when we found out she had first been robbing banks. That just wasn't the Peggy Sue I knew, or anyone knew. Now, as time has passed, I wonder."

"Like?"

Pete hesitated. "Was it really Peggy Sue they shot and killed?"

"What makes you think that? You identified the body."

"I know I was the only one left to do that since our older sister died from cancer, but there's just this little bit of nagging doubt I may have been wrong, I may have made a mistake."

"Go on."

"You know how she took four bullets to the chest and one to the face and then fell face-first into the pavement?"

"That's what the report said."

"Peggy Sue had a small birthmark on her face. I couldn't find it, but it was in the area where the bullet struck, and she did the face plant, so I wrote it off to face trauma, but now I'm not so sure."

"Interesting. The report did make reference to the double mastectomy."

"Yes, the body was missing both breasts, but two other things were odd. She had a scar on her knee where she wrecked her bike when she was young. Her knees were boogered up from where she fell, but I couldn't find the scar. Again, like I said, I think I was in shock and just wrote it off to the trauma from the fall."

186

Roger said, "I can see how that could happen. Anything else?"

"One last thing. The body had a little butterfly tattoo on her right ankle. I didn't know she had one, but there seem to be a lot people didn't know about my sister."

"So, you think she may be alive?"

"I seriously doubt it, but as I said, these things keep circulating in my brain. I wish I could say for sure. I think most likely she and Cowboy Gene are both dead. But I wish I was 100% sure for complete closure."

"Pete, if she did have a bug out plan, an escape plan, where would she go?"

He put his hand to his chin and stroked it thoughtfully. He looked at something distant and spoke, "She talked about wanting to live on the West Coast and wanting to watch the sun go down every evening."

"Like the Tampa-Clearwater area?"

"No, not the Florida West Coast. The Pacific."

"California, Oregon?"

"I think you're getting warm, California, yes, but not in the US. There'd be the chance someone would recognize her and report her to the authorities. I'd bet on Mexico, Baja California."

"Baja California? That's over 700 miles long from north to south. That'd be a big area to look in."

"No, if I know anything about Peggy Sue, she doesn't do things halfway. She'd go all the way. If she's alive and to be found, she's in a motor home on the beach overlooking the Pacific at land's end at the very southern end of the peninsula watching the sun go down every night. That's where I'd look for her if I was going to look, but I won't. I don't want to know that bad."

"And if someone did find her there?" Roger asked.

"I hope they'd tell her that her family loves her and misses her. And then I hope they'd get in their vehicle, drive away, and forget they ever saw her."

The two men sat in silence for a few moments and sipped on their beverages of choice. "Good water," said Pete.

"Spring water from West Virginia. Best I know of." He paused, "Is there anything more you'd like to tell me?"

"No, I don't think so. I've probably said more than I should already."

Neither man said anything for some time.

"Guess I better be going," Pete said.

"Yeah, I think your business is done here, Pete."

"What are you going to do with this information?"

Roger said, "I don't know," but each knew Roger would be taking a trip out west soon. "Thank you for coming. Does this help put your mind at peace?"

"Only a little. Complete closure is what I'd like."

"I understand how you feel. Now that the donkey knows who you are, you'll be safe walking out."

"Thanks for hearing me out. I'll be going now."

Roger rose from his chair, and the two men shook hands. "Thanks for sharing the information with me. Have a good day."

"You, too." Pete exited the door and walked to his truck, unmolested by the donkey. His vehicle soon disappeared in a cloud of dust from unpaved Canaveral Flats Boulevard.

Roger stroked his mustache as he thought. A question nagged him now, a question he would never have believed probable if not totally impossible only an hour ago. And he knew he was going on a long road trip very soon. If not, this question would haunt him as long as he had breath. He had to know.

Chapter 30

One Week Later

"Lester, I sure want to thank you for offering this ride to the airport. Parking would have cost me a fortune. And I'm glad it's you watching over my place and critters while I'm gone."

"Roger, it ain't no problem for me. You know all you had to do was ask, and it was as good as done."

"Thank you. Here's twenty bucks upfront to take care of the tolls and your gas. Seems like Orlando's full of tolls."

"Yup, no tolls in our county. Those crooked politicians in Orange County like to squeeze every dime they can out of the people there."

"Lester, don't you think they'll ever come to their senses and vote them out?

Lester laughed, "Always bet on stupid. It's a great way to double your money."

Roger laughed, too. "There should be plenty of food for the cat and dog and donkey should be good with the grass on the property. If not, get him some hay. Put it on my tab, and I'll settle up when I get back."

"And when's that?"

"I'm not sure. Could be as short as a week. Could be as long as three weeks. If I don't come back, I've got a handwritten will in the cookie jar on my kitchen table if needed."

"Roger, you're makin' this sound like it could be dangerous. What are you up to?"

"I'd rather not say. This could be a wild goose chase for nothing, but on the other hand, there could be some problems."

"And you're not gonna tell me what they are, are you?"

"Nope. You're gonna have to trust me on this one."

" What if Bill or someone asks about you?"

"Just tell 'em I got antsy and had to go on walkabout. You know, the wanderlust bit me, and I had to go."

"Whatever you say, Roger. You're a big boy able to make up your own mind."

"Thanks for trusting me on this one, Lester."

Lester drove west on the Beeline. "River's looking low. Gator's been eatin' good on the critters they catch when they come for a drink."

"Seems like it's been about this size every time I've seen it since I've been here. Cows could cross it and not get their bellies wet."

"You should see it when we get lots of rain. It can be a mile wide and seem to go on forever."

Roger said, "Someday, I'll see it, but today ain't that day. Guess I'll have to wait."

"Yup. The marsh along the St. Johns River's open range and a few ranchers keep their cattle out here."

"My home state has a little bit of open range along the South Branch of the Potomac River valley, but I thought all the rest of the open range was west of the Mississippi."

Lester said, "It is. Learn somethin' new every day. Didn't know about it in West Virginia."

"Yup, you can learn somethin' new every day if you just listen and pay attention. Hey, Lester, I just realized something. You ain't sayin' 'Sir' to Bill Kenney any more. What's up?'

"Oh, you mean because I used to be grateful for him and his dad saving my family when I was young from the guys in the sheets. Well, Bill asked me not to. It was embarrassing him, and he goaded me into stoppin', so I did, just to make him happy. I'm still grateful there're people who stand up to injustice."

Roger said, "Guess you'd know about that."

"Yup, it can be hard not to be bitter, but bitterness will eat you up from the inside. Did I ever tell you about my wife and her family?"

"No, I never heard you talk about her, ever."

"Well, Roger, it's about time I do. Her name was Esther, and she was a fine woman. Drove me crazy some times, but don't they all?"

"Very true, Lester. I can remember one day when I came home, my wife was mad at me, and I had no idea why, so I asked her why she was mad, and she said I should know. I told her she needed to tell me what she was mad about, or I might apologize for the wrong thing, and then she really got mad. She wouldn't talk to me for several hours. Actually, I was kinda enjoying the peace and quiet. Whatever it was, she forgave me and started talking again. And you know, to this day, I have no idea what set her off."

"Probably better not knowing."

"You're probably right," Roger said.

Lester laughed, "Yes, sir. That sure sounds like a woman. But you know, there ain't no viable substitute, so I guess we got to figure out somehow to live with them. We're stuck with 'em for better or for worse."

"Yeah, she sure made a monkey out of old King Kong, and I don't think somethin' better gonna come along."

Lester chucked, "Nope, but I bet there were times ole Adam wished he could have his rib back."

"I believe you're right on that. Now, what was it you wanted to tell me about your late wife?"

"Oh, yes, my late wife. That lady, she came from hardy stock. Ever heard of Robert Smalls? He was either her grandfather or great grandfather. I can't remember which one right now."

"Can't say I have. Who was he?"

"He was born a slave in South Carolina before the Civil War and worked the docks of Charleston where he became an experienced seaman. He got assigned to steer a Confederate Navy vessel, the Planter, for them. The crew was a few white men and mainly slaves. He earned their trust completely. One night when the ship was full of heavy guns and the white officers went ashore, the enslaved men under Small's command hijacked the vessel, picked up their families, and sailed past a number of Confederate checkpoints. Smalls fooled them by giving the correct signals while dressed in the captain's clothes. When they met the Union ships, they hoisted the white flag and surrendered the ship and its guns to the surprised Union sailors.

"He enlisted in the Union Navy, fought in many battles, and because of his bravery under fire, was

194

promoted to captain of the same vessel he had been a slave on. He went on to learn to read and write and, as a war hero, used his influence to see education was available for former slaves.

"After the war, he entered politics and served as a Republican in the South Carolina legislature and then was elected to the US House of Representatives. He stayed active in public life into the 20th Century. And the plantation he was a slave on? He bought it after the war and lived on it till his death in 1915. I've been to his grave. His monument is inscribed with these words, 'My race needs no special defense, for the past history of them in this country proves them to be the equal of any people anywhere. All they need is an equal chance in the battle of life.'"

"That's quite a story, Lester."

"It is, but life ain't always fair, and not everyone wanted black folk to get an equal chance. Things went backwards with segregation and Jim Crow Laws. It wasn't till WWII that things began to change. I think I told you how the country was desperate for men during the war."

"You did. You told me how they ran out of white men to fight, and then they reluctantly dipped into the pool of black men available," Roger said.

"They'd already got the white women workin' taking the manufacturing and administration jobs while the men were away, but they still needed more people, and there at the bottom of the barrel was the black women. Can you imagine what it was like for them, Roger?"

"No, I can't." He sighed. "They had to be very tough."

"Like cut nails. My future wife-to-be tried to get in the Army Nurses Corps but was denied because they were only allowed to take care of black soldiers, and there were very few in combat in Europe. Still, under pressure from the NAACP, they admitted fifty-six black nurses in 1941, and that was under their quota system. Esther got her training and, in 1943, was sent to Liberia to care for segregated units of black soldiers. She said she never knew there was so many black folks in the world as there were in Africa. By the end of the war, about 500 black women served as nurses in the Army. Though she was happy to help her country even if it treated her as a less than equal, she was glad to serve. She did say that this unequal treatment was a real morale killer for many blacks in the service she ran into.

"After the war, she served in the segregated hospitals in the local area and as a midwife. She delivered many a child in the little shotgun houses you find around here." He stopped. "I miss her."

A tear rolled down the furrowed cheek of Lester, and he wiped it away. He looked awkward and uncomfortable, but Roger tried not to notice.

Roger said, "Hey, that sign said we need to turn here for the airport."

Lester took the exit, and soon Roger was getting out at the airport with his bag.

Lester said, "You sure you don't want to tell me anything more about this trip?"

"No, I said enough already. I have to go."

Lester stuck out his hand. Roger took it but pulled the old black man to him and hugged him. Then he stepped away. "There are times you feel like family, Lester. I know everything will be fine while I'm away."

"It do, Roger. Everything be fine here. You go do what you got to do. Don't worry about nothin' here."

"No need to with you watchin' over it." Roger smiled, tipped his hat, and walked into the nearby building.

A serious expression came to Lester's face. "And I hope everything goes fine with you." He got in his old truck and drove away.

Chapter 31

"Over here, Roger, I'm over here."

Roger scanned the crowd at the San Diego Airport for the person calling his name, but he didn't see the familiar face he was looking for.

"Over here, Roger."

He saw a blond-haired woman moving toward him. "Linda?"

"Don't you recognize me, you ole ridge running hillbilly?"

Roger smiled, "Why, it is you. You've changed a little since I last saw you."

"You haven't changed at all, except for a few gray hairs in that hard head of yours."

"That's the Linda I remember. Full of piss and vinegar. I need a hug."

She threw her arms out, and they embraced.

"So good to see you," he said.

"And you, too, Roger, though there's a little more of me now to see."

"I wasn't going to say anything, but yes, there is."

Linda said, "Yeah, life's been good. I've filled out a little."

About forty pounds. Roger said, "Let's get out of here and catch up on old times."

"Sounds good. How was your flight?"

"We hit some turbulence over New Mexico, and several people lost their lunch, but several beers help to keep me pretty mellow."

"Yup, that's the Roger I know."

"The only other surprise was the landing at the airport. I thought the landing gears and wheels were gonna hit some downtown buildings on the way in. We were dropping like a rock on the approach, and then the crosswind hit."

"Welcome to Lindbergh Airport. That's pretty normal. Some days it's even worse with the crosswinds. You brought back my first memories of flying here for the job interview. I remember my white knuckles. And it was a turbulent day. My car's nearby in the parking lot. Let's go. Hungry? I got a place in the Gaslight Quarter I know you'll love."

"What are we waiting for then? Let's make like Bugs Bunny and hop to it."

She smiled. "That's the Roger I know."

They walked a short distance, and she stopped at a convertible muscle car. "Get in. It's mine."

Roger grinned. "Nice car. Looks like you done alright, Linda."

"'69 Boss Mustang with 302 cubes, 290+ horsepower, and a 4 on the floor. It can go 0 to 60 in 6 seconds or less and do the quarter-mile at around a hundred miles an hour. It'll kick ass, and there's not much around here that'll even come close."

"Linda, I believe. I wasn't hungry till you mentioned food. Now I'm starved."

"Okay, let's get going."

She paid the parking fee, and they got on a downtown street with a light on every corner. At the second light, four boys joyriding began to hassle them. "Hey, look, grandmaw's gotta drive grandpaw around. What a waste of a hot car."

"Try to ignore them, Linda."

"I'll try."

They caught every red light for five blocks, and the taunts from the boys grew louder and meaner. "What a waste of a hot car. Grandmaw ain't got hot in decades, and grandpaw may have a Mustang, but the old stud's now as useless as a gelding."

200

"I've had about enough of them, Linda."

"I got an idea, Roger. Trust me on this."

"Okay."

She revved up the engine a little. "So you babies think you're men. Go home and suck on your momma's tittie."

"You hear that, Leroy? You hear what she called us?" came a voice in the car.

Linda said, "Yeah, you hear that, Billy? You children ain't even potty trained. You're still in diapers, newborns."

"You hear what that old woman called us, Billy? Are we gonna take that?'

Linda said with disgust in her voice, "You guys ain't nothin' but a bunch of uncircumcised Philistines."

The boys looked at each other puzzled. One said, "Billy, I think we've been insulted, and big time. What are we gonna do about it?"

Linda revved up the engine. "Yeah, Billy, what are you gonna do about it?" She revved the engine again, longer and louder this time.

The driver of the other car did the same. Linda turned her head to them and grinned from ear to ear. She nodded, and the other driver did, too.

The light changed to green, and the race was on. Wheels squealed, and the tires tore at the road as the smoke billowed from them. An expletive slipped from Roger's lips as he was thrown back in the seat. Linda pulled out in the lead. She went through the gears like a champ as the other car got further behind. Without warning, she downshifted and let off the gas. The other vehicle, still accelerating, passed them by, and the ecstatic boys hooted and hollered.

"What are you doing?" asked Roger.

She smiled. "You just wait."

They crested a small hill doing the legal limit on the four-lane highway. Off in the distance, a police car with lights flashing was pulling over a car full of boys. They caught up, and as they passed, Roger and Linda waved and smiled to the unhappy boys. One gave them the finger, which only made the couple smile wider and laugh.

Roger said, "You played them like a fine violin. That was amazing."

"I knew that cop usually sat there hidden by the rise just waiting for speeders, and I thought I'd help them out."

"Linda, I knew you were a sly dog in the old days, and it seems you've kicked it up a couple of notches."

"Thank you, Roger. And as I remember, you weren't a slouch back then, and I think you've probably gotten badder."

"Why, thank you, Linda. How much longer to the restaurant?"

"About two minutes. You'll like this place."

They went down a side street, took another right, and pulled into an open parking spot in front of Croce's Restaurant and Jazz Bar. "We're here."

Roger looked at the mural painted on the building. A curly-haired man with an overgrown mustache and a cigar in his hand looked down on them. He looked at Linda. "Croce's? As in Jim Croce, the singer?"

"Yep, that one. Bad, Bad, Leroy Brown. That one."

Roger grinned, "This is gonna be good. Let's go inside. It's getting a little cool out here."

They walked into the street level restaurant in the five-story building on the corner. A woman greeted them. "Can I help you?"

"Table for two," said Linda.

"Can we get a spot where we can talk?" asked Roger.

"Certainly," the woman said. She took them to an empty spot, and a waiter quickly came and took their drink and food order.

"It won't be long," he said.

Roger excused himself and went to the restroom. When he returned, the mixed drinks and their meals were there. "That was fast," he said.

"This place is known for its quick service. Looks like the music is about to start. How about we eat, listen to the show, and talk afterward?"

"Guess so. It pays to be flexible."

"And I know just the place," Linda said.

"Sounds like a plan."

Chapter 32

The meal was excellent, as was the entertainment by some local band Linda had heard of. After it, they left and drove to Linda's place. The cool breeze felt good and helped clear their minds from the many mixed drinks they had consumed.

"So what brings you to California, Roger? It liked to bowled me over when I got your phone call. Why are you here?"

"It's hard to explain. It's some old business and a need to answer a nagging question. I need to have an important conversation with someone."

She smiled, "And who would that someone be?"

"Someone from my past. That person may not even exist anymore. I'm not even sure where to locate that person."

Roger thought he saw her face fall, but she tried to cover it up.

"What's the person's name?"

"Cowboy Gene. Ever heard the name?"

"Can't say I have. Why do you want to find him?"

Roger made no effort to correct Linda. "As I said, it's old business and a need to answer some important questions."

"And where do you think this person who may no longer exist can be found?"

"Baja, near the very end."

"Roger, Baja California's almost 800 miles long. The road down there is bad. Why, it's about a thirty-hour drive, if you don't stop or break down. You don't have a car, and it's in a different county. This must be pretty important."

"It is."

"And if you do get there, how will you know where to find him. It's a big area, one you're not familiar with, and it would be really easy to miss him."

Roger said, "I know it would, but I think I know where Cowboy Gene can be located. It should only take a couple of days to figure out one way or the other."

She shook her head. "This idea of yours is crazy. Maybe you haven't changed as much as I thought. You came over 3000 miles across the country, and now you're going 800 miles into a foreign country to chase down a person who may or may not be there and may not even exist."

"Linda, that about sums it up nicely. Can I count on your help?"

"Roger, you know me too well, of course, even if you're certifiable."

Roger gave his best Sam Elliott grin.

"Stop it, Roger. You know you're irresistible when you do that."

He laughed. "So, how can you help me on my crazy plan?"

"I wouldn't drive it. Takes too much time. You'd have to get to the border, cross it, find a car in Tijuana, then drive all the way down there, and not get mugged on the way, gringo."

"So what do you recommend?"

"I know a man, kind of a friend I met through my work at the zoo, who flies regular charter flights from San Diego to La Paz down near the south end. I'll check and see if he's going any time soon. He could arrange for you to have a car waiting and all the proper papers are signed off on. You get down there and don't have proper insurance, get in an accident, and get taken off to jail until they get around to sorting it all out whenever that is, and they're not known for expediency."

"That would be super if you could arrange that. I'd need a car, oh, maybe three days. If I can't find Cowboy

Gene by then, I don't think I ever will. Time to move on and come back to the USA."

"Sounds like a plan, Roger. Hope it works out."

"Me, too."

"Couple of more things, Roger."

"What's that?"

"If you see a sign that says Baño, it means bathroom."

Roger nodded. "Yeah, I can see how that would be helpful."

"And Linda in Spanish means pretty."

Roger grinned. "Now, why am I not surprised?"

She chucked. "I picked up a little Spanish while I was gathering specimens in Mexico."

"Thanks, Linda, it'll help. My Spanish isn't that good."

They pulled up to a gate.

"We're here," she said.

"The sign says, 'Deliveries, San Diego Zoo,' Linda."

"They provide me with housing. One of the perks of the job, and it gives them an extra set of eyes on the park.

You wouldn't believe some of the weirdos who find their way in or the crazy stuff that goes on here."

"Linda, how about telling me one when we get in, okay?"

"Sure thing."

She punched in a set of numbers in a panel, and the gate opened. She drove in, waited for the gate to close, and then drove up a slope to some townhouses that looked like they should be on the African Serengeti. "This is it. This is where I hang my hat."

"Interesting place."

"Let me show you my special place, Roger."

"And tell me those stories. I love stories."

"Follow me," she said. She walked up a steep path and then climbed some steps as steep as a ladder.

Roger looked up as she climbed in front of him, and memories of the pleasures they had shared as lovers crept into his mind. She disappeared over the top. Her face reappeared. "What are you waiting on? Come on. We're here."

"I got distracted. I'll be right there, Linda."

He quickly climbed the stairs and found himself in a desert wonderland. "Wow, what is this place?"

"My favorite place, the Baja Jungle. If you fly down, you'll miss a lot of this that's only found about halfway down the Baja peninsula."

Roger said, "I know what some of the plants are, some of the cactuses and succulents, but what are those weird things?" He pointed to a plant that looked like a twisted telephone pole covered with small limbs and leaves.

"That's a boojum."

"Like Lewis Carroll's story?"

Linda said, "That's right, only the boojum in his story was a weird animal."

"And this is a very weird plant."

"It is, and I was one of the ones who collected them and others down in Mexico when they still allowed it. I'm glad we got as many as we did when we could. That's how I gained my knowledge about Baja."

"Not bad for a girl from the hick town of Springs, Pennsylvania."

She laughed. "No, I'm full of surprises. And that tall cactus that looks like a saguaro, but actually a cousin is called a Mexican Cardon. Now, they do grow in the south end of Baja, but not the boojum. That's only in the middle."

"This is a mystical place. I can see why you like it, Linda."

"It's my happy place to escape when the world starts to close in on me. I can come here, and my problems slowly melt away."

"You were gonna tell me some stories?" Roger said.

"Yeah, I was. Animals can do some strange things, but people are even stranger. We had some lovey-dovey Nubian donkeys, Napoleon and Josephine, here at the zoo, and they often behaved like the randy animals they are. One day, they were passing the sausage, as we keepers like to call the activity, in front of a school group, and the ladies there took offense and made a stink about it. We temporarily separated them, but boy, oh boy, did they put up a fuss.

"Their plight made it to the local papers, and after a petition was circulated that gathered 7,000 signatures, the amorous couple was reunited to live and couple as they wished. This story had a happy ending."

Roger said, "I know a little about amorous donkeys and the trouble they can cause."

"An escaped con once took up living in the zoo. He stole bananas from the elephants, once ate one of our tortoises, broke into vending machines, and slept on the roof of one of the huts. His own stupidity finally caught up with him. One of the elephants cornered him, and he barely escaped. He was very happy when the elephant keeper got Jumbo away from him, and even happier to go back to the safety of jail."

"I can understand that. Heard a similar story back in Florida."

She paused, looked to the side, and placed her hand on Roger's. She sighed, "You going to spend the night in my bed like we did back in the old times?"

Roger said nothing for a moment. "No, I don't think so."

"It's because I've gotten fat, isn't it?"

"No, Linda, it's not that. I remember the good times we had in the sack and out of it, but time has moved on, and I'm different. You see, shortly after you left, I met the woman who became my wife. We were married several years when she and our small son were killed in a car wreck. I drank myself into a stupor daily to fight the pain. I was a mess, and it's just been lately I've been able to get out of this depression I was in. Then, I found I had a son I didn't know I had living in the same county I was in. He got hit by a truck and almost died. My life has been an out of control roller coaster since I last saw you."

"How's your son now?"

"Almost fully recovered. All this has given me a different perspective on life. Linda, I know there's someone out there for you, and it's not me. The next woman I want to sleep with will be my wife. How's that for an old-fashioned cornball explanation?"

She smiled and kissed him on the forehead. "You're a good man, Roger Pyles. It's getting late. I need to make a phone call for a flight for you. You can sleep on the couch. And no hard feelings about any of this. You'll always be my friend."

"Thank you for that affirmation. I got a question for you."

"What's that?"

"Uncircumcised Philistine. Where did that come from? Those boys were totally baffled, as was I."

"Roger, I never told you this, but my dad was a Mennonite preacher. It was something he used to call a lowlife type."

"Really? I didn't know you were a PK."

"Yeah, I'm a preacher's kid. Got a brother who followed in Dad's footsteps, but me and my sister are the hellions in the family. Dad died a while back. I talk to my brother now and then. He always tells me he's praying for me and sis."

"Linda, think I got a bunch of people praying for me, too."

"Can't do any harm. It's my brother's way of saying he still cares."

Roger said, "I can understand that. You know, it's getting' late. Let's turn in. Tomorrow will be here in a jiffy."

"It will. Follow me."

"Can I tell you a funny story about my wife?"

"Sure, Roger. Indulge me."

"Kay wanted to make me a special pie, and she got this recipe from a friend who claimed it was to die for. It almost was. She put it in the oven and set the timer. Well, we got frisky and then fell asleep. The smoke alarm woke us up. The pan had overflowed into the oven, and the whole house was full of smoke. We opened up the window to get the smoke out. A neighbor saw the smoke and called the local volunteer fire department. It was just around the corner, and they showed up pronto. We were barely dressed. To say the least, it was something I'll never forget. It was special, alright."

"Roger, you're funny. Don't change. Any more stories?"

"Nope."

"Okay, now follow me. We'll go the long way. It's not near as steep and easier on the knees." They walked down the winding path to her townhouse apartment, making small talk. She showed him the couch and got a pillow, some sheets, and a blanket from a closet. After she made a brief phone call, he had a flight to La Paz tomorrow morning. Roger took a quick shower and lay down in the darkened apartment. He'd made it through another day successfully. What would he find in Baja? His stomach churned a bit. Where was Cowboy Gene?

Chapter 33

The flight from San Diego to La Paz lasted a little over two hours from takeoff to touch down. The weather was good with unlimited visibility. Roger enjoyed looking down on the Baja Peninsula, the Pacific Ocean, and the Gulf of Cortez.

Security at the airport was lax for the people coming in on the private flight. The pilot, Linda's friend, gave Roger good instructions on how not to look like a gringo and get ripped off by the auto rental company; however, it was unnecessary. The young woman at the desk kept looking at him and grinning as he filled out his paperwork. Infatuation flowed from her face, and she spoke to him in English with only a slight accent.

"Mr. Elliott, I really like your movies."

"I think you've got me confused with someone else, miss."

"No, Señor. You don't have to pretend you're someone else. I really like your cowboy movies, especially the one with Tom Selleck, who is your brother. You fought for different sides in the American Civil War."

"The movie you're thinking of is called *The Shadow*

Riders. But I assure you, my name is Roger Pyles. I just look like Sam Elliott. This isn't the first time I've been confused for him."

"Whatever you say, Mr. El-, Mr. Pyles. You put down you would be renting the car day by day. Do you have any idea how long you will be needing it?"

"Two or three days should do it. I'll return it here to the airport."

"Please remember our hours are 8 AM to 6 PM. We're not a major airport like you're used to, Señor."

"Could I have a map of the area?"

"Certainly."

She gave him a one-page map, and Roger studies it carefully. "Where would be the best place to watch the sunset south of here?"

She thought for a moment. "Cabo San Lucas at land's end is nice. The bay is beautiful, and the stone arch is worth seeing. Further north is Playa La Cachora, and then there is Cerritos Beach. What exactly are you looking for? Wild to civilized?"

Roger smiled. "I'll know it when I see it."

"Certainly. Señor. Have a pleasant stay while you're in our area."

"I hope so," he said. "I got someone to find that may not want to be found."

Her face dropped. "You really aren't Sam Elliott."

"Nope, and this ain't no movie."

She looked surprised, turned away, and said no more.

Roger showed the paperwork to a short, stocky young man outside who pointed him to a mid-size vehicle. He threw his bag in the trunk, opened the side door, and got in. Whoever rented the car before him had been short. His knees were against the dash, and he quickly found the seat adjustment and pushed the seat all the way back.

"Much better," he muttered. After adjusting the mirrors, he familiarized himself with the instrument layouts. Roger remembered once renting a car in a foreign country and having an unpleasant experience. It was getting dark, and he couldn't find the light switch. Lucky for him, that car had the owner's manual in it, though it was in a foreign language that didn't use Roman script, and there was no English version. A few cryptic drawings he could decipher got the lights on, but it was too dark for his comfort by that time, and he had no desire to repeat that fiasco.

He found his way to Highway 1. Traffic was lighter than he expected. He stopped at a fast-food restaurant for a quick meal and questioned the cashier about the way south to Cabo San Lucas. There were two ways, Highway 19 and Highway 1. Highway 19, which hugged the west coast, would be more direct. Still, Roger wanted to see the eastern side of the peninsula as he realized he would probably never return to Baja California Sur again, so he took the other road.

He frequently stopped to enjoy the many magnificent views and take pictures. The normally three-hour drive took him twice that, and he arrived in Cabo San Lucas in need of a break and hungry. He got a room at the Holiday Inn, where he also had supper in the hotel restaurant. There was a large selection of places to stay and eat, but he chose a place familiar to him. After a meal of pork chops, he noted a placard for sunset cruises to see the land's end at the Arch of Cabo San Lucas.

"Señor, would you like a ticket?"

Roger said, "Could you tell me more, please?"

"The bus to the boat is leaving very soon. It's a two-hour tour on the water."

"How much?"

"Thirty-nine dollars."

"How big is the boat?"

"She's one hundred and eleven feet and has two levels. Food is available as well as drinks."
Roger said, "Drinks sound good to settle my stomach and system. No food. I've been known to visit Captain Ralph."

"You get seasick, Señor?"

"Yeah, I've been known to feed the fishes."

"The water should be fairly calm tonight, two to four feet."

"Okay, I'm in. I'll take a ticket."

"Good choice, Señor. You won't regret it."

Roger smiled, "I hope not."

"You'll make a memory."

Roger laughed, "That's for sure. One way or the other. Here's the money before I talk myself out of it."

"Good choice."

Roger grinned. He took the ticket from the young man and walked to the bus, which was nearly full. A fat woman sat next to him and seemed to have no interest in small talk, so Roger enjoyed the sights on the way to the marina. They arrived in about ten minutes and made their way to the boat, the La Sinera. A bare-breasted mermaid was painted next to the name.

Roger boarded the vessel, got two Corona beers, and headed for the upper deck. He found a seat in the front row. The bottom level began to fill up, and people began to find their way to the upper level. A senior age couple sat down next to Roger. The man spoke to Roger, "Good evening to you, young fella."

"Good evening to you, too, Sir."

Roger stuck out his hand, and the men shook.

"My name is Glen. This is my wife, Kathy."

"Glad to meet you, ma'am. I'm Roger. I live in Florida now. Moved down there from the Western Maryland area a few years ago, but I grew up in West Virginia."

"Where in West Virginia?" Glen asked.

"A little town on the south side of the Potomac across the river from Cumberland, Maryland, no one has ever heard of, Fort Ashby."

"I know where Fort Ashby is. Years ago, when I was a young buck, I worked for a mining company located in Morgantown. They offered me a job in Wyoming near Gillette with better pay, and I took it. Went from hunting white-tailed deer to hunting mule deer. The weather was a little colder, but not much. I retired two years ago, and we moved down here. This was our go-to vacation place, and we said, what the heck, let's make it home, and so we have."

Kathy said, "We love it here and will never go back."

Glen said, "We bought a house in a nearby town and loved it."

"This is my first time in Baja. They tell me the sunsets are spectacular down here on the south end." Roger said.

"You're in for a treat. Whatever you've been told is pale compared to the real thing."

The senior man asked Roger, "How long are you here?"

"Two or three days, I think. The number one item on my agenda is to see beautiful sunsets. Where's the best place for that?"

"You'll see a good one tonight."

Roger said, "I'm looking for a place on the land on the Pacific side where I can watch the sun dip into the ocean and disappear. I'm hoping to see the green flash. I saw it once in Florida."

"There's a lot of good places off of Highway 19," Kathy said.

"I need a spot with a road big enough for a motor home and a place to park it," Roger said.

"Not too many places like that," Glen said. "Lots of good beaches, but limited access. Any suggestions, Honey?"

"I'd suggest Cerritos Beach," Kathy said. "That would be the best one. It's stunning and kind of wild-looking still, even with the Hacienda Cerritos Resort set up on the rocky hill that sticks out into the ocean. It's a great place to catch the sunsets. It's our favorite place, isn't it Glen?"

He smiled. "It is. It's beautiful there. Other than the resort on the hill, there's not much development. Lots of driftwood. The beach is packed sand, but there are lots of big boulders sticking out of the sandy beach."

"That sounds exactly like the place I'm looking for," said Roger. "Thank you so much."

The boat lurched a little and began to nose out into the bay.

Glen said, "Looks like we're underway. We never get tired of going on this cruise. We may see some dolphins, too, and the sunset is spectacular. It's my favorite out here."

Kathy said, "It is, but my favorite's Cerritos Beach. You see them both and then make up your mind."

"I will," said Roger. "Thank you for your advice."

They made small talk during the cruise. Roger bought beers for himself and Glen. He got Cokes for Kathy. She wasn't a drinker.

The cruise by the rock sea Arch of Cabo San Lucas was spectacular, as was the sunset that night. Both men were well lubricated by the time the boat returned to the pier. Roger was glad he didn't have to drive. The bus ride back to the hotel went quickly. He found his room on the third floor, took a long shower, and then thought about tomorrow. He'd check out the area, enjoy the sights, scope out the beaches with particular interest on Cerritos Beach, and be at Cerritos an hour or two before sunset. If Peggy

Sue, a.k.a. Cowboy Gene, was alive, he believed he'd find her there. He felt sure he'd know for certain tomorrow, but he was prepared to be disappointed.

Roger wondered how she'd react if indeed she was there, but he thought he already knew. Still.

Chapter 34

The next day, Roger checked out every beach between Cabo San Lucas and Todos Santos. There was only one he could get to till he got to Migriño. There were several between there and Todos Santos, but only one impressed him as a place Peggy Sue would come to and watch the sunset, Cerritos Beach. It took him most of the day to do this.

He drove up to the Hacienda Cerritos and found a place to park. He had his choice of spots as the lot was pretty empty. *Not a good sign. I would have thought the lot would be full. Good food means a crowded lot.* He considered his situation. *Probably not tourist season.*

He walked to the main entrance and saw a man behind a counter on the left.

"Which way to the restaurant?" Roger asked.

"We have several, Señor. The casual one is on your left. The American style is to the right, and the deluxe is on the second floor. Which one would you like?"

"The casual one on the left, does it have a view of the beach? That is looking south, correct?"

"It is, Señor."

"That will work out fine."

"Do you need a room for the night, Señor?"

"No, just a good and filling meal," Roger said.

"Very good. Follow me."

Roger did, and a well-dressed waiter greeted him. Roger told him he wanted a table with a view down the beach. One was open, and they went to it.

"Do you know what you would like to drink, Señor?"

"What's a good Mexican beer, young man?"

"Modelo is a local favorite. We have many. It's your choice."

Roger said, "Then make it a Modelo, no, get me two."

"Very good, Señor."

The waiter left, and Roger scanned the menu. The ropa vieja seemed to perk his interest. The young man soon returned with two beers. "Here you are, Señor. I see you're looking at the menu. Have you made a selection?"

"The ropa vieja sounds interesting. Is it good?" Roger asked.

"Excellent, but everything at the Hacienda Cerritos is excellent."

Roger took a sip of the beer. "This is good."

"That's why it's a local favorite."

"I notice you rattle off to the people here in perfect Spanish, but I see you have no accent when you speak to me in English. Could you explain that?"

The young man smiled. "My parents moved to San Diego from Baja before I was born. I grew up there hearing both languages since I was little. My family got tired of the rat race in Southern California and moved back, so here I am."

"Interesting. What's your name?"

"Eduardo."

"Good name. I'm Roger."

He extended his hand, and they shook.

"What brings you to Baja, Señor?"

"Business. Eduardo, I'm kinda hungry. Could you put my order in, please?"

Eduardo took the hint and left. Roger looked down at the beach to the south side. Yes, if he was going to find Peggy Sue, this was the place. He watched the surfers catch the wave. Driftwood lay among the large rocks that punctuated the beach in numerous spots. Roger finished his first beer. "Yup," he said out loud to himself. "This is the most likely place."

"Señor, is everything okay?"

Roger jumped. "Oh, sorry. Just thinking out loud. Sometimes I do that when I'm lost in thought."

"No need to explain. Here's your meal. Enjoy." He turned but stopped. "Would you like another beer, Señor?"

"Sounds good, and get me the bill, please. I can't believe how quick the service is here."

"I'll get you the beer. Mr. Roger, you're lucky today. You should see what a madhouse this place is when it's tourist season."

Hungry Roger tore into the meal, and it was delicious. The second beer was soon gone, and Eduardo returned with another beer and the check. "Here you go, Señor. How was the meal?"

"Excellent. I hope I can find this when I get back home to Florida."

"You should. It's a traditional Cuban meal, and you have lots of Cubans in Florida."

"True, Eduardo. Thank you. I'll definitely remember this night."

"Very good, Señor. Have a good night, and thank you."

Eduardo left, and Roger continued eating his meal between gulps of beer. He stopped in mid swallow as he saw a woman in a sundress and carrying a lawn chair working her way down a path from a parking lot on a small bluff to the beach. *Peggy Sue. That has to be Peggy Sue.*

He quickly finished his meal and beer and watched the woman. She picked a spot near a large rock, one of many sticking out of the beach, unfolded the chair, and sat facing the setting sun. Roger looked at the bill. All seemed in order. He left enough cash for the bill along with a substantial tip for Eduardo, then got up, and headed for the door.

Eduardo saw him and spoke. "Is all well, Señor?"

"It is. Business calls. I left cash for the meal at the table. Any extra is yours."

"Thank you. I hope your business is successful, and you return again soon."

Roger said, "I doubt if I will ever return, but I would like to if the opportunity comes up again. Thank you for your service. My business is calling."

"Have a nice night, Mr. Roger."

"You, too."

Roger stopped at the bathroom and got rid of some of the beer before making his way to the rental car. In five minutes, he'd be at the beach parking lot, and in five more, he'd know if his quest would be successful.

How will she react? What will she do when I confront her? He thought he knew, but there was always that element of uncertainty.

He started the engine, backed the car out, and started down the road from the Hacienda Cerritos to the road that led to the beach parking lot. He'd soon get the answers to his questions, and he hoped it all worked out for everyone, the living and the dead.

Chapter 35

Roger took a right off the main road and headed for the beach down the unpaved lane. The parking lot was about a quarter full. He picked an open spot next to a small Holiday Rambler motor home, parked, got out, cautiously looked it over closely.

No one seemed to be in it, and the tags were local, Baja California Sur. He noticed dolphin themed curtains hanging in the trailer windows. Looking through a window he believed to be where the kitchen was (he was right), he saw a little glass menagerie of dolphins and a newspaper laying on the table, *Florida Today*, the local paper of Brevard County, Florida. This had to be it. He'd hit pay dirt. Now he had to head for the beach and find Peggy Sue. His stomach churned a little, and he wondered how this meeting would go, but he'd gone this far, and there was no turning back.

The path to the beach was well worn. A couple of young men still wet from the ocean and carrying surfboards passed him going the other direction.

"How was the action today, fellas?"

One said something to the other in Spanish, who replied to Roger in English with a heavy accent, "It was a good day to surf, amigo. Are you a surfer?"

"Not really, but I live near Cocoa Beach, Florida, and I see them catching waves there all the time."

"You're missing half your life, my friend. Have you been to Ron Jon's?"

Roger said, "Yes, I think I have one of their T-shirts somewhere around my house."

"If you're not here to surf, you must be here for the beautiful sunset."

"I saw one last night from Cabo San Lucas. Spectacular. I'm meeting a young woman who should be on the beach waiting for me. She's about 35 and wearing a bright sundress."

The second man said something in Spanish to his friend. He nodded and spoke to Roger. "My friend says he saw your lady friend. He understands English much better than he speaks it. You can find her just past the rocks. She's down the beach to the left."

Roger said, "And she's sitting in a beach chair if I know her at all."

"That she is, amigo."

"Thank you, guys. I'll try to surprise her."

The men laughed. "It's pretty open on the beach. It will be hard to surprise her."

Roger smiled, "We'll see. Thanks, guys. Have a great night."

"You and your lady friend, too."

Roger grinned, and the men went their separate ways.

Looking at the position of the Sun, Roger guessed there was about an hour of daylight till the Sun would sink into the ocean. He followed the path through the scrubby beach shrubs and rocks and emerged onto the beach. Sitting about one hundred feet away in a beach chair and wearing a bright yellow sundress, sat a woman smoking a cigarette, and she sure resembled Peggy Sue. Roger walked in her direction. As he grew close, he saw her put her right hand under her dress. "Excuse me. I think I may know you."

"You can stop right there, whoever you are."

"My name's Roger Pyles."

She shifted in her seat.

"And I believe your name is Peggy Sue Tallman."

"I think you have me mistaken for someone else, young man."

"I don't think so. Too many things tell me otherwise."

She said nothing, so Roger continued, "I came all the way from Brevard County in Florida to find you. I had to know if you were alive or not."

She remained silent. He said, "I knew you preferred Holiday Ramblers, and when I saw the dolphins and the *Florida Today* Newspaper in the motor home, I was certain I'd found you."

She smiled slightly. "I wondered if this day would ever come. How did you know I'd be here?"

"Everyone thought you were dead, even your brother Pete who identified the body as yours. He said he thought it was you, but the longer he considered it, the bigger the red flags got. Pete shared these doubts with me recently. After careful contemplation, I came to the same conclusion, and I had to know if this case was over or not."

"Good old Pete," she laughed. "I should have known he'd figure it out."

"Don't be too hard on him. He says he still loves his sister. I think he just wanted this to be over, finalized, and done."

"I love him, too, and I also want this over. Roger, I've got a gun strapped to my leg under my dress."

"I thought so. I saw you reach under there." He paused. "Are you gonna shoot me? Put an end to it all?"

She remained silent for a moment. "No, I'm not going to shoot you."

Roger let out a deep breath. "I was hoping you'd see it that way."

"I carry it for self-protection. Some people would think I'd be easy prey, a woman traveling alone in a foreign country. I never used a gun when I robbed any of the banks, and I'd rather this gun never be fired in anger. I fired it at a local range several times. Works good up close, but ain't worth squat at a distance."

"Short barrel?"

"And small enough for my hand."

"Yeah, a gun like that's only good for up close and personal," Roger said. "Mind if I sit down?"

"Why not? Pull up a rock or sit on the sand. Your choice."

"The sand will do fine." He sat down. "Pete mentioned if you were anywhere, it would be at the end of the world watching the sunset. This place fits the bill."

"Good detective work, Roger Pyles. What do you want to know? I'll tell you everything." She took a big puff on her cigarette.

"Peggy Sue, how do you know I won't report what I've found to the authorities back home?"

"I don't, but I want to talk. There're some things I need to get off my chest, and now would be a good time." She stopped and looked to the west. "Sun'll be down soon and be resurrected in the morning. This is my favorite place in my world. I have a spot in an RV park nearby, but you can find me on this beach every evening, except for when the weather's bad, which isn't often."

"Okay, I have some questions? Why? Why did you do it?"

She looked off to the setting sun and said nothing. Roger waited, and she shifted in the chair.

"I often wondered if I could do it. Pull it off, get away, and no one gets hurt. The first one was kind of a lark, and then it got rather addictive. I think I know how Butch Cassidy must have felt. I never carried a gun, and no one ever got hurt, you know?"

Roger said, "Yeah, you were very clever and smart. You had the FBI, state and local police, all chasing their tails, completely buffaloed."

She smiled, "I did, didn't I? It got to be kind of a challenge, me versus them, and they didn't even know who they were looking for. I sure had them fooled, and not having a front porch helped out a lot."

"How many banks did you rob?"

She took another puff on the cigarette. "I don't know. I lost count. A bunch of them, but you always remember the first and the last."

"Were they all in central Florida?" Roger asked.

She shook her head. "Florida is all I'll say. If you heard of any outside of the state, it wasn't me. I know there were some copycats."

"What did you do with the money?"

"I spent it. I used a lot of it to pay Mom's medical bills. Pete helped with those, but I never told him how bad it was. Sometimes when we got low, I'd rob another bank and then lie low until we needed more money."

"What was the last bank you robbed?"

"A bank in Eustis. I hit the jackpot there. That's what I'm living on right now."

Roger asked, "So what will you do when you run out of money?"

She looked down. "Not going to happen."

Roger pondered that statement before asking his next question. "So, if the last bank you robbed was in Eustis, who robbed the bank in Cocoa?"

"Cowboy Jean."

"Cowboy Gene?"

"I need to explain. You know I had a double mastectomy. Cancer runs in my family. While at the boutique I got mastectomy bras at in Rockledge, I met another woman named Jean, that's J e a n. She was an old friend, and I hadn't seen her in years. She'd recently had the same procedure and needed proper bras for her new condition, no boobies. Jean looked enough like me to be my sister, some say twin sister, but as best we could tell, weren't related. We had coffee and compared notes and soon became very good friends again. We talked about everything-cancer, men, family, life, and girl stuff, of course."

"Did you tell her about robbing banks?"

"After I found I could trust her with my biggest secrets, I told her about it. She was shocked and fascinated. I told her everything. At last, I'd mastered the art of bank robbery and was quitting soon. I learned a lot in prison about how to do better and not get caught from the other gals there. Thank you, State of Florida.

"Find a bank near a highway. Case the place. Know it like your home. Remain calm. No running or hurrying. Violence is the sign of an amateur. Be an actor and stay in character. It's an art. My hearing aid was attached to a police scanner, and I knew if a silent alarm had been pulled. You learn by doing. There's no manual, and you can't teach it, but it looks like she forgot something I told her and slipped up. Jean was intelligent enough to get herself into trouble but not smart enough to get herself out of trouble or stay out of trouble. And you got to learn from your mistakes, but she never got the chance. She slipped up and paid dearly. No one is born a great bank robber or thief. You have to learn to be careful, plan, and hone your skills."

Roger said, "You should write this all down for people to know. The FBI would love this story. You could tell it at seminars."

She shook her head, "No. Not sure I want people to know. Information like this can be dangerous. Roger, I've told you about all there is to tell. You could do it. I'll leave that in your ballpark."

He said, "Interesting. I'll think on that."

She said, "I was already in Baja when I saw the story on the front page of *Florida Today* about the Cocoa bank robbery, the chase, the shootout, and the death, some say the murder of Cowboy Gene. More like suicide by cop. It was a shock to think she had actually tried to do it. You did know the newspaper will send it to you wherever you are in the world? It costs more, but I'm glad I did it."

"How did you know what to do?"

She said, "I called them from a payphone, told them I was a former resident now living in Mexico and wanted to get the paper. They told me what to do, and I sent them cash so that I couldn't be traced. The name was fictitious. It's what I've been using lately."

"And the motor home you had in Florida?"

"After my big score, I needed to get the heck out of Dodge, so I sold it to her. Guess she never changed the title into her name."

Roger said, "Yup, another reason they thought it was you as Cowboy Gene."

"The paper published the note she left. I saw how she signed it, Cowboy Jean, J e a n, and then erased her name. It was that apparent to me even from the grainy photo in the paper. I think she wanted some credit in a way for the robbery, and for the authorities to close the case on Cowboy Gene."

"It almost worked."

"Yes, it did, almost, if not for super-sleuth, pain in the butt, Roger Pyles."

"I've been called far worse. So what should I do with this new information about Cowboy Gene?"

She said, "Do what you want to. It won't make any difference." She took another puff.

"You know smoking's not good for you."

"Won't make any difference."

"What do you mean?"

She sighed, "I've already got a death sentence."

Roger showed surprise. "You could possibly get a few years in prison after a trial."

"I'm not going back to prison. You see, my cancer's back. I started having problems soon after I got to Baja. I found an American doctor living in La Paz, who's a cancer specialist. He got tired of the rat race in Los Angeles and escaped here. It's pretty common. Anyway, my cancer's back. It's spreading, and there's nothing that can be done about it. It's just a matter of time before it gets me."

"I'm sorry."

"Don't be. Everyone has to die sometime. I thought I'd have a little more time, but there's no guarantee for tomorrow. I always wanted to go to heaven, but I didn't think I go one piece at a time. I had a hysterectomy, too, and my gall bladder out. We all fall apart and wear out. I always wanted a husband and a family, but that just didn't happen."

"I don't know what to say."

"Then say nothing, Roger Pyles. You know, when I sit here and watch the sunsets, sometimes I think of taking a long walk into the ocean and never coming back. It might be best if I did."

They sat in silence as the Sun dipped into the ocean. Finally, Roger spoke. "I think I need to be going." He got up.

She said, "So, what are you going to do about Cowboy Gene?"

"I don't know. I could just walk away, not look back, and forget the whole thing."

She smiled. "I know you'll make the right decision. And no hard feelings, Roger."

Roger said, "No hard feelings here, either. I know you'll make the right decision."

"Thanks for listening, Roger, and understanding. And one last thing, Roger."

"What's that?"

"If anyone had to catch me, I'm glad it was you. Keep up the good work. The world needs people like you."

Roger said nothing for a moment as he digested her words. "Well, Peggy Sue, guess this is goodbye. I'll walk you to your motor home if you like."

"No, I think I want to remain here and watch the Sun drop all the way down to the ocean tonight. Sometimes, you can even catch the green flash as it disappears."

"I've heard that. I'm going now. Peace be with you always."

"And you, too, Roger Pyles. May you have a long life. My days are numbered."

Roger wasn't sure what to say. He thought for a moment, looked at her, and said, "Bye."

"Goodbye, Roger. It was good to see you again. Thank you for your concern."

With that, he pivoted and walked to the parking lot. There, he glanced back to the ocean and saw Peggy Sue standing on the beach with the waves lapping at her feet. The sun was setting rapidly. Only a little sliver was still showing, and then it quickly disappeared. A green flash pulsed on the horizon and was gone as quickly as it had appeared. It couldn't have lasted even two seconds.

He looked toward the beach where he had last seen Peggy Sue, but she wasn't there. Darkness grew rapidly as he scanned the ocean for a yellow dress, but he saw nothing. Roger Pyles got in his rental car and drove off, never looking back.

Chapter 36

Two Weeks Later, Canaveral Flats, Florida

Roger watched the car stop in front of his trailer. A tall man got out, and Roger recognized him as Pastor Nassey. K9 got up and growled. "It's okay, K9. He's a friendly. It's not Bill."

The dog snorted at the hearing of Bill's name and then gave a welcoming yelp as she saw the pastor coming down the path to the old trailer.

"Hey, Roger. How's it going?"

"Oh, pretty good. Yourself?"

"Same here. Permission to come on board."

"Pastor, come on in. You're always welcome here."

"Thanks."

Roger said, "Tea?"

"Sure. It's another hot day in Florida."

"Aren't they all? Take a seat, pastor. Be back in a jiffy."

The pastor sat down, and K9 went to him. He stroked her head and back. "Good girl. You keeping Roger out of trouble?"

Roger came out of the open door with two teas. "She is and keeping troubles of all kinds away."

"Like Bill Kenney?"

K9 growled.

Roger smiled. "Yeah, all kinds of riff-raff, including Bill Kenney."

K9 growled again.

"What brings you to my neighborhood today, Pastor?"

"Got a new family coming to church, and I thought I'd stop in and get to know them better. They bought the old Tallman place. The brother finally got a clear title to it. Peggy Sue died without a will, so that tied it up, and then the state took a big chunk. Make a will, Roger, if you don't want to enrich the state needlessly."

"Thanks for that, Pastor. You never know when you're gonna die, and I'd like to see everything I got goes to whoever I want, and not the state."

Pastor said, "Yeah, I see the situation a lot." He sighed. "You know it's hard for me to fathom that Cowboy Gene was Peggy Sue and living among us unseen."

"You're right on that, Pastor. You could have knocked me over with a feather when I figured that out."

"It's even harder to believe she's actually dead. What a way to go."

"That's a mouthful. I still find the facts hard to believe."

Pastor said, "Whatever was she thinking?"

Roger nodded, "Some things are hard to explain. Maybe we'll never know the full story."

"Very true."

"What are the new owners doin' to the place?"

Pastor said, "Not really that much. Some new paint and fixtures. Cleaning up the yard that had been let go. That's about it."

"Yeah, it amazed me how Peggy Sue was able to keep it up so well and care for her mother at the same time."

"She was a smart gal in some ways."

Roger said, "Yeah, in some ways. You got time for a philosophical question today?"

"If it's not so involved. Yeah, I got a little time. What's on your mind?"

"Suffering. Why is there so much suffering in this world?"

"Roger, people have asked that question throughout recorded history and probably before that. Can I give you the nutshell version answer?"

"Sure. Go ahead."

"There just is a lot of suffering. You got to deal with it. It's how we react to it. It can make you bitter or better. Some people want to be happy all the time, and if they're not happy, they ask does life have any meaning. There's nothing wrong with trying to be happy, but often people think if they're unhappy, then they're a failure. Some even take their own life. Happiness can be like a shallow boat in a very rough sea-tossed aimlessly about by the waves. You got to have purpose in your life to survive the low points and come out better. Roger, do you know who Aleksandr Solzhenitsyn is?"

"Who doesn't? The man who survived and documented the Soviet gulag prison system."

"That's him, but you'd be surprised how many don't. He rejected that the pursuit of happiness was a proper goal in life. Let me paraphrase him, 'The pursuit of happiness is a pitiful ideology done in by the beat downs in everyone's lives.' Imagine what his life was like in those Siberian political prisons. What gave his life meaning wasn't trying to find happiness, but surviving whatever the authorities threw at him and living to record and tell the world of what had happened in the gulags. Also, thoughts of his family and personal responsibility. With these, he survived the horrible trial with his spirit not only intact but triumphant. That's what got him and many others through tough times.

"And one more thing. When asked why all the disasters had fallen on Russia, he replied, 'Men have forgotten God.' I believe that's the reason why mankind is so troubled; mankind has forgotten God. How's that for an answer in a nutshell?"

Roger looked a little dazed. "Glad that's the nutshell version. There's enough meat in those words to choke a hungry lion. I'm goin' to have to take it one small bite at a time. You said a mouthful and a half."

"I told you I didn't have much time. You ruminate on that. I've got to get to another visitation up the road. One of the dear old lady saints of the church has taken ill and may be on her death bed. I need to go comfort her, Roger. You know what's funny, when I visit people like her in her condition, often they comfort me. They're at peace and eagerly awaiting going home."

Roger said nothing for a moment. "Well, guess you better get goin' then. Thanks for stoppin' in. You're always welcome here."

"And thanks for the tea. Got to go. Be seeing you, Roger."

"Take care, pastor. Bye. Be sure to close the gate. Donkey's been known to escape."

"Will do."

Pastor Nassey soon disappeared in his car, leaving Roger to his thoughts. He wondered where the cat was. *Hadn't seen her in a day or so. Hope a coyote or something else hadn't got her.* He thought about what the pastor'd said. Heavy duty stuff like that required serious consideration over time.

K9 barked, and he saw Lester Johnson coming through the gate. "Well, well," Roger said. "Looks like I'm a popular guy. Another visitor."

"How's it going, Roger? You good for company?"

"Sure, Lester. Come on down."

The old black man walked to the porch and said, "It sure is hot. Got anything cold to drink?"

"Coke, tea, and beer. What'll you have?"

Lester grinned, "A beer sounds fine."

"Then a beer it is. Have a seat. Take a load off your mind."

"I'll do that."

Roger went in the trailer and got two beers. He gave one to Lester, who thanked him.

"Lester, thanks for feeding my critters while I was away. Looks like everything went well here."

"It did. I found your message on the answering machine a while back, telling me you'd returned. Did everything go fine for you out west? Did you get your questions answered? Find what you wanted to know?"

Roger ignored the question for a moment, took a big gulp on his beer, and seemed to be staring at something a long way off. He said nothing.

Lester waited, but Roger remained silent. "Roger, did…"

Roger cut him off. "I heard you, Lester. I knew you'd show up and ask about my trip, but I don't have any more of an explanation now than when you took me to the airport. You're just gonna have to trust me on this."

Lester nodded. "I know the feeling. Sometimes people ask me about the war. What was it like? It brings up memories I'd like to forget. I pray they never find out. Things they're better off not knowing. Is that kinda what you're telling me?"

Roger said, "It is."

"I won't ask again."

"Thank you, Lester."

"I got a confession to make to you, Roger."

"What's that?"

"I ate one of your chocolate chip cookies every day while you were gone. Ain't none left."

"Lester, I left them out for you to find. I meant them for you."

"Now you done ruined it, Roger. They tasted better when they were stolen."

Roger laughed. "Ain't that the truth? When me and Bill were boys, we used to steal watermelons from the patch of a local farmer, Mr. Wagoner. Ain't nothin' sweeter or tastier than a stolen watermelon."

Lester laughed, "I wouldn't know. I'll take your word on it."

"Sure you will. How's things going for you?"

"Fine as can be. And you?"

"Well, Lester, I've been busy, but I'm between assignments now. I'm sure something will come up soon. It always does."

"You're not going on walkabout again, are you?"

"No, got that out of my system for a while. Something will come up."

Lester nodded. "I'm sure it will. I'd bet on it. We live in interesting times."

"We sure do. It won't be long. I can feel it. I can even taste it.

The end

WANT TO READ MORE?
Braddock's Gold Novels – Braddock's Gold, Hunter's Moon, Fool's Wisdom, and Killing Darkness
Florida Murder Mystery Novels – Death at Windover, Murder at the Canaveral Diner, Murder at the Indian River, Murder at Seminole Pond, and Murder of Cowboy Gene

Murder of Cowboy Gene is the fifth in the expanding *Florida Murder Mystery Novels*. Each book in the series is written as stand-alone novel. Readers say he keeps getting better. All of Mr. Heavner's nine books can be found on Amazon as ebooks and paperbacks. The first book, *Braddock's Gold*, is also available as an audiobook from Audible at Amazon.

WANT TO HELP THE AUTHOR?
If you enjoyed the book, would you help get the word out? Please tell others about it. Word-of-mouth advertising is the best marketing tool on this planet.

A good review on Amazon, Goodreads, or elsewhere would help with the author being able to keep writing full time. It doesn't have to be long. Thanks.

SIGN UP FOR JAY HEAVNER'S NEWSLETTER
With this, Jay will occasionally keep you informed with new books coming out and anything else special. Feel free to email him at jay@jayheavner.com. His website is www.jayheavner.com. He loves reader feedback.

Made in the USA
Middletown, DE
20 September 2021